Spirit of Fire

Spirit of Fire

The Tale of Marjorie Bruce

Emmerson Brand

Prologue

This is not a diary; this is proof that my father was a hero.

A retelling, if you wish to call it that. But not a diary. I was young, and I still am, but sitting by the hearth now surrounded by what is left of my family, I ken the mistakes I have made, and I need you to understand what exactly happened to us, the Scottish, during the many years of English occupation.

My mother died in childbirth. I never got the chance to meet her because I was too busy screaming my way into this war-stricken world. I may have cried out for her, but my memory does not span that far back into my past. My father certainly cried for her, either in his sleep or in his mind. I might not have been able to see it, but I knew he was grieving. Every time he glanced at me.

Talk of the village was that I was the spitting image of my late mother. If anything, for much of my earlier life I was sure I resembled a rodent. My large front teeth were mostly to blame, but once my blossoming began my face moulded around them. If I remember correctly, that began around the age of three and ten years.

My father, Robert the Bruce, was laird of our clan at the time we joined the rest of the Highlanders in war. As a laird, he had been given the task of producing healthy male heirs to take his position once he passed. At the time of my mother's death, I was the only child he had legitimately created. Elizabeth de Burgh became his second wife five years later, in a ceremony at a small parish church.

When we joined the war, I had not yet welcomed any brothers or sisters, although if the time came that Father was granted another title, my stepmother would have to dwell even further on the thought of giving him a male heir to secure the Bruce line.

Chapter One

From the journal of Marjorie Bruce
26th of March, 1306

Today was such an exciting day. We left early this morning on horseback into Scone for my father's coronation. Old Bishop William de Lamberton was there performing the ceremony that made my father the newly crowned king of Scotland. My stepmother Elizabeth was anointed as the king's consort, and I was not forgotten either. I was the last to be crowned. I am finally royalty, like Aunt Isabel.

I was not born a princess, so I have not the vaguest idea of how to act. Supposedly we have to act proper and roam the courtyards with servants by our sides and guards protecting us from everything that causes us even a little harm.

Soon after the coronation, we received a letter from my father's military advisor. It seems that he is to go to war very soon. I do hate it when he does, as it gets very boring in the household. There is no one to lighten up its doorways. As well, there is always a notion that he may not return, perishing in battle, and that thought is not appropriate for such a young girl like me to have.

Elizabeth, my stepmother, is seventeen. She has long, delicate red hair, much like that of a fox. Father always says that red hair is the trait of the Scots, and soon the world will be overrun with Scotsmen alike. Elizabeth's body shape has not yet been ruined by the marks of childbearing, and everything about her is tender, gentle, and soft.

I cannot compare her to Mother as I had never met her, not once. I prefer to believe that she was as beautiful as Elizabeth is. It is quite upsetting. I was her only bairn, and I do not have friends except for the poor slave girl Emmeline.

I like not to think about Emmeline much, because when I do, it causes me a great deal of sorrow. The lass is sixteen years of age, yet she is bedded every night by the drunken men of my father's army. They do not care about the women they bed; they just want their pleasure. Countless times she has been pregnant, and all but four of her children have died in infancy. The warriors each give her a few coins for her troubles and never speak to her again. They do not even spare a glance for their children.

My father is yet to enlighten me on my marriage arrangements, although I expect that I am to be wed to a son of one of the noblemen within my father's court. I do not care much to dwell on the thoughts of my future and what it may have in store for me.

Although Emmeline has lost her pride, she still proves to be a dutiful mother to all four of her children. I enjoy aiding her by looking after her mischievous children as she spends her waking hours at task.

Marjorie Bruce

30th of March, 1306

Father left two days ago to meet his army at the holds in Irvine. In a month he is to go to war. Pray to the Lord that he will survive.

Emmeline is always happy when the army leaves Ayrshire. I mentioned to her yesterday morn that I would make it my personal quest to find her a suitable husband just after the household healer advised her not to fall pregnant again. The stress of another bastard child would be the death of her. A husband will take care of her, and she shall live in happiness.

Elizabeth had received orders from my father that we were to travel to Norway to visit my aunt Isabel and cousin Ingeborg. My cousin is a year younger than me, and her late father, King Eric II, died when she was two. We are to leave tomorrow, and I gather that my father had more in mind than a polite visit. Emmeline and her children shall sail on the same boat as I, and Elizabeth and I shall share a cabin, so Emmeline can have her own. I truly do not mind sharing, and neither does Elizabeth. I believe we shall both enjoy the trip together.

At this moment, I am sitting by the hearth in Emmeline's quarters watching over her children, who are all fast asleep. It is late at night, and I should be getting some rest as well. The youngest, Sorcha, is prone to stirring in the night. Her small form is as beautiful as an angel's; she has her mother's soft, delicate hands, and a fiery spirit. Although I am only nine, I cannot wait to become a mother and hold a delicate infant in my hands.

Emmeline has just arrived home, and she has given me a parcel containing red berries to take home to Elizabeth. I shall not intrude anymore, and I shall leave her with her children for the night.

Marjorie Bruce

7th of April, 1306

The boat docked in Oslo just last week, and the trip was less than delightful. I had not realized that I was one of many who would get seasick repeatedly. Being cooped up in a cabin when the ocean was in turmoil did not help at all, and the food was less than grand.

I was glad to rid myself of the boat. It smelt like sick, and Emmeline's off-spring were constantly retching over the side of the boat. For a lady who is used to a garderobe, I found the alternative quite unsettling and difficult to get used to.

It was embarrassing to ride into the capital in rags, hair all matted with grease and a face covered in dirt. After a short ride on horseback, our company arrived at Aunt Isabel's palace and were greeted by several guards, all speaking Norwegian. I had no knowledge of this foreign tongue, and consequently my curiosity awoke.

I must say, the palace was majestic. The long corridors were illuminated with torches and music and I wandered down , running my hand along the walls and glossed furniture, luxuriating in the warmth. This Scandinavian household seemed to reflect a tranquil and placid persona, much unlike Turnberry Castle's rough edges and bustling hallways. Never had I such a love for a house, and yet it was not mine.

My bodily reaction to the journey was so severe that it kept my stomach churning for two more days. I spent those hours in a large bed in a guest room. I slept and retched in a regular pattern, the nightmares of the tumbling sea taking over any rationality I once had. A fever came on the second day, but broke soon after. I was out of bed by the third day and ready to meet my relations.

There was to be a grand congregation of nobility that night in the main hall. I ambled towards my stepmother, shy of everyone else. I did not ken them, and they were all foreign figures to me. I had not been introduced to Aunt Isabel prior to our arrival, so you could only imagine my surprise when she laid a warm, delicate hand on my shoulder, interrupting my progress towards Elizabeth. I turned to see a tall, slender figure standing above me. Dressed in an elegant emerald green shawl and dress, Aunt Isabel looked down upon me with a quizzical look, obviously thinking about something that had crossed her mind.

I looked over to find Elizabeth's face in the sea of nobility surging around me. I felt like a doomed ship stuck in a whirlpool of men and women alike. When I caught her eye, she noticed that Isabel was with me and hurried quickly over.

Curtseying politely, she smiled up at Father's sister. "Dowager Queen Isabel, how pleasant it is to be in your presence."

I curtseyed alongside, following Elizabeth's actions. "And I am Princess Marjorie de Brus, your majesty."

"My dear Marjorie, I am so pleased to finally meet you. King Robert has told me plenty in our usual correspondence!" Aunt Isabel exclaimed, grasping my hand and holding it in hers.

"Is cousin Ingeborg attending tonight?" I asked, curious about this cousin that I had not yet met.

The queen dowager smiled softly. "Ingeborg is, yet she knows little of the Scottish tongue so it may be hard to communicate." At that moment Isabel gestured a well-dressed servant forward to the group we were standing in.

"Alvar, please show the queen and the princess into the drawing room, and we shall discuss the business we have intended to."

Turning back to us, she smiled. "Alvar here is the only guard in my company to be fluent in the Scottish tongue. It is quite refreshing."

The dark-skinned servant moved forward and parted the crowd so we could follow him into a smaller room adjacent to the large hall. Aunt Isabel strode in soon after with a girl whom I assumed was my cousin Ingeborg. The small girl resembled her mother almost wholly, and her buck-toothed smile greeted me on arrival. The women sat down synchronously and folded their gloved hands across their laps as a sort of formality. I could not help but do the same.

"I have made plans for my dear daughter in the near future," Isabel said slowly. "She is to wed an earl by the name of Jon Magnusson when she comes of age."

Ingeborg sat there dumbly, not understanding a single word of the conversation unfolding in front of her. I wondered whether she had been told of these plans.

"We should get you married soon, young Marjorie," Isabel proceeded. "You need a good man to break you in and teach you the ways of the housewife. In fact, I've got the perfect nobleman here. Royalty, he is."

Before I could open my mouth, Elizabeth intervened. "She is only nine, Isabel. She will not marry until she reaches fourteen. Those are her father's orders, and she is not even a woman yet."

"And you are seventeen, Elizabeth," she retorted. "Shouldn't you be bearing children yet? Brother Robert will be getting anxious for an heir soon."

Turning to me, she scowled. "Do you have any idea what this means for you, Marjorie?"

I shook my head, utterly confused. Elizabeth placed a hand on my shoulder and tried to reason with the queen dowager. "Marjorie is young. She does not understand the formalities quite yet. I do not understand why she should need to worry herself with them either."

In Isabel's eyes I saw pity, although I did not know whether to feel grateful or degraded. "You have the title of princess now, Marjorie, and you are the eldest child of the king of Scotland." She paused her lecture to stifle a sigh. "However, what you do not understand is that as soon as Elizabeth married your father, your right to the crown was put into question. Any offspring by Elizabeth will have first priority, and you will have nothing."

Elizabeth stood there in shock. Straightening her shawl, she stormed off, leaving me standing there in front of my aunt. I felt completely speechless and utterly terrified as I left the bright hall, no longer feeling the warmth that I was so sure I had felt before. I wanted Father so badly. Certainly he wouldn't agree with Aunt Isabel.

I ran through the dim halls in search of either Elizabeth or Emmeline. Entering the guest room, I hoped someone would in there, but the room was dark and empty. The servants' quarters were the next place I ransacked, the whole time my spark of hope fading. I knew deep down that I wouldn't find anyone I knew in this massive palace.

Marjorie Bruce

8th of April, 1306

In the end my instincts told me that they had gone down to the docks and left me behind.

As I ran barefoot towards the docks, I tripped over a large protrusion from the ground. I fell onto the floor and smashed my face against the rocks. Hearing everything crack at the same time, I knew then that this would have to be the death of me. And it truly felt like it the next day.

But to my relief, I felt the hands of a man pick me off the ground. At this point I was on the verge of consciousness, teetering in between two worlds. He carried me wordlessly down into the docks, obviously aware of my intentions.

"Princess Marjorie, can you hear me? Emmeline told me to find you and take you back to your galley." I could not understand most of his accented Scottish, but that one word caught me in my tracks. Emmeline. My guess was that this man was seventeen, young enough to have associated with my friend within the three days we were in Norway. However, that did not matter. I needed to get to Elizabeth.

The docks were large, too large for my liking. My sight came back to me, and I remembered all that had just occurred: Aunt Isabel, the fall and the black unconsciousness.

The man put me down onto the cold ground and asked me what ship I had arrived on. I looked around into the growing twilight. Right at the end of the docks, bobbing amidst the blue-grey water, was Father's boat, the *Eithne-Searlaid*. Torches were aflame on board the boat, and I knew that they were readying to leave. When I pointed the *Eithne-Searlaid* out to the tall servant, he whisked me into his arms and ran down towards where my family stayed.

The servant, who I had now recognized as Alvar, propped me up onto the deck and asked me to inform Emmeline of his arrival. I walked along the side of the magnificent beast, carefully holding onto the side as I said a prayer to Saint Oda for light so I could see where I was treading. As I turned the corner, a gruff voice stirred behind me, and as I realized that I had woken a sleeping guard, it was all too late.

He picked me up by the collar of my nightgown and thrust me towards the open sea, thinking I was an intruder. I screamed and shouted, and Elizabeth ran onto the deck with a look of horror on her face. I had just escaped death, and it had found me again and put me in its grasp. She grabbed me by the waist and hauled me on board. I was sopping wet from the spray of the ocean.

I was crying. Never had I been so scared before. I spent the night in Emmeline's cabin, and I told her of Alvar. Afterwards she looked for Elizabeth to ask for permission to let him board. She was overjoyed that Emmeline had found someone who cared about her at last, and, with no hesitation, she let him board. Alvar, whom I could see more clearly now, was ever grateful to me. I told him, that, as long as he was happy, he could do whatever he wished.

The guard who had almost ended my life was now raising the sail, and that meant that we were going home.

Marjorie Bruce

17th of April, 1306

The *Eithne-Searlaid* landed back in Ayrshire yesterday because we had no intention of staying in Norway any longer. Not in Aunt Isabel's presence.

Our dismal journey to Oslo was countered with Father's arrival back in Ayrshire. I went to greet him inside the courtyard, and he had brought Elizabeth and me a rose each. He is very kind and thoughtful, but when he is angry he flies into the most horrible rages. Once Father had settled and dismissed his men, Elizabeth told him about Aunt Isabel's interrogation, and he stood there in a sort of trance before smashing the vase in front of him. He asked me whether it was true, and I mumbled a yes.

There is one thing I need to tell you before I continue on with the story. If I hear people talking quietly, I usually eavesdrop. It is deceitful to do so, I know, but I simply cannot help missing out on anything that sounds interesting. So that is how I found myself sitting at my father's doorway later that night, trying to hear the conversation within.

This time, the voices were hushed, and I could only hear a wee bit of their conversation. It turns out that Father did not go to his holds at Irvine, as he had told me, but to a bishop instead. My dear father had sinned, although I do not ken how nor why. He had been excommunicated. It is a long word for a wee child of nine, and I do not ken yet what it means. I must ask Emmeline tonight, just before she goes out with Alvar.

I think Father somehow knows that I was listening to their conversation this morning because he was acting unusually quiet. I must somehow seek the truth without acting suspicious.

I have time to waste, so I must tell you as much as I can understand about the war between England and Scotland.

The English king, Edward I, or "Longshanks" as many call him, is a horrible and terrible tyrant. Although I have never met him myself, I plan not to. When you hear of him, all you think of is greed, greed, greed. This Longshanks has the throne of England, yet he wishes to also take over Scotland. The tyrant is unjust and does not even deserve to wear a crown. My father was only the earl of Carrick last year, and his friend, William Wallace, was a warrior. Sir William only wanted freedom for Scotland, nothing else. He did not want a title, he did not want to be king, yet Sir William fought for that freedom.

Edward did not want to give it to him. Instead, last year, he captured Sir William Wallace and sentenced him to be hanged, drawn, and quartered. It is not appropriate for a young girl to be talking about such things. It is also not appropriate for such innocent people to die such horrible deaths. Sir William adored me, and I called him Uncle. It pains me to even think of him anymore as it is still fresh on my mind. I shall only refer to Edward by his true name: "the Tyrant."

The past king of Scotland, John Balliol, was too weak to be king, and there was no one to inherit it from him. So a priest called Dun Scotus presented the Scottish nobles with a plan, merely an idea. It was the idea that the rightful King of Scotland could be chosen by the people, not by the traditional royal succession. This meant that Father, along with John Comyn, were both eligible to be King.

You may wonder how a wee girl may ken all of this, and it is because Father's dear friend, William de Lamberton, a bishop, educates me in Scottish politics and history. I must say, I enjoy my classes with him thoroughly, and I have knowledge and a great curiosity for these subjects. The bishop has mentioned that I am one of his most prized pupils.

Marjorie Bruce

Chapter Two

From the journal of Marjorie Bruce
   17th of June, 1306

I had asked Emmeline about the word that my father had used when he was speaking to Elizabeth. She had said that it meant to be banned from the church, to be labelled as a fugitive who had sinned terribly and to not be welcomed in the church or in Heaven. The excommunicated person was damned.

She had asked me why I was questioning her about it, and I told her that I had read it in one of the bishop's texts. I did not want Emmeline to find out about my father. This information was too dear to me.

I decided to discuss it with the bishop because I needed to know more. I waited until Elizabeth and Father were asleep before sneaking into the bishop's quarters. I was barefooted and shivering in my nightgown as the sea breeze was ever so cold. I chose to go at night because the bishop is always awake until the early hours of the morning.

In the glow of the firelight, I could see the bishop working tirelessly away on a script, only ever pausing to dip his feathered quill in an ink pot. I ambled my way over to the elder, and once I had reached him, I nudged his shoulder. He turned to face me, his eyes glowing with delight, and he gestured for me to sit down. I didn't waste a moment and immediately plunged forward with my question. I told him how I had overheard the conversation and how Emmeline had told me what "excommunicated" meant. His face showed concern when I asked about the sin my father made. He was reluctant to tell me, but I would not leave without an answer.

Marjorie Bruce

18th of June, 1306

Father had insisted that we should leave Ayrshire immediately due to English raiders a few hundred leagues south of our castle. Dumfries was also under attack at the time we evacuated Ayrshire. Raiders are extremely dangerous, so we are to travel along the coastal road to Perth. The road was treacherous, and I had no intention of falling under my stallion, Ciaran, as that would be the death of me. This meant that the ride was long and tiring, and I swear that I have never ridden so much in the nine years of my life. At the very moment that I write this account, I am sitting under a boulder overlooking the stormy ocean. Father is talking to Elizabeth and the bishop quietly, Emmeline and Alvar are feeding the horses, and Sorcha is playing a game with her siblings. Even though I am only nine, with the knowledge I possess I feel older, I feel powerful. Even though Elizabeth, the bishop, and my father were most likely discussing secrets, I did not feel the urge to eavesdrop. Strange.

I must leave this account soon as we have to continue onwards. We will not stop until the day is finished. I have heard rumours that my father's army has been residing in a village to the west of Perth and that we were to meet them there for a reason that was beyond my knowledge.

We reached Methven just before nightfall, and our band took cover in a small inn. The town was almost dead, and only a number of houses still existed. Methven must have been ravaged by the English earlier in the year. Houses had been turned to rubble, livestock were slaughtered, and stray cats were picking at the dead. I couldn't bear to look at anything, so I kept my head covered underneath my cloak.

I tethered Ciaran in the stable of the inn and went to join my stepmother in the house. In one corner, the bishop was praying with Emmeline, Alvar, and the children, while in the other, Elizabeth and Father were whispering quietly as though they knew something the rest of us did not.

The bishop is calling me over for prayers now, I must go.

Marjorie Bruce

21st of June, 1306

I only have a little time before we leave, but I ought to get this message written urgently. I must account for what I witnessed on the early morning of the nineteenth.

After prayers, everyone settled down to rest. Or so I thought. I could not bear to sleep after I had seen all the carnage and destruction that once was the city of Methven. I would have had nightmares. Bishop William was asleep, Elizabeth, Emmeline, Alvar, the children, everyone but Father and I. Thinking I was fast asleep, he stumbled over to my stepmother and kissed her gently on the forehead. He made his way over to me, tripping over a wooden stool in the process. He kissed my forehead, and I closed my eyes so he would not know I was awake. Then Father did the strangest thing.

He took off his nightclothes and replaced them with his battle armour. Father was not headed to battle? I watched him pick up *Molreach*, his longsword, and sheathe it. He turned to us, made the sign of the cross, and wandered out of the room.

I immediately sprang out of bed and ran to the window that overlooked the streets of Methven. Father's army was mounted on horseback, swords and shields at the ready. When the army started to march north into the woods with my father at the head, I decided to follow, being the inquisitive lass I am.

I stumbled down the stairs of the inn and ran out through the doorway. Cats were still roaming the street, and I no longer felt safe. This was a bad idea. I tripped over dead bodies, rotting cattle and pieces of rubble as I followed my father and his army into the woods. Never had I been so scared.

I crept into the woods, and as I sheltered underneath a tree, there was a scream of rage, a blast of a trumpet, and the battle began.

From where I was sitting, I couldn't see Father, but I hoped to the Lord above that he was alive and had survived the first cavalry charge. The English advanced, led by one of my father's enemies, Valence. He is one of the Tyrant's best military commanders, and he made the first kill. Blood sprayed everywhere, a Scottish body flew across the woods, and from the minute the battle had started, I could tell that the Scottish would lose

I was frightened, and I acted foolishly. So foolishly that I could not even begin to reason why I ran to Father. He was in the middle of the battle, and I would either be trampled or mutilated. I saw the Bruce shield and his sword, but before I even crossed into battle territory, an English archer caught me and pushed me over to Valence, who had just finished a slaughter of soldiers. When he saw me, he grinned greedily.

"With this little girl," he spoke in fluent French, holding me up by my neck, "we've already won the battle."

Valence turned to face his soldiers. "We've already won," he yelled to his soldiers, who stopped their slaughter to listen to their leader.

Valence unsheathed his sword and held it to my neck as he turned to Father. He stopped and stared at Valence, then looked down to me.

"Your daughter could be safe asleep right now," Valence started, "but she was foolish and decided to follow you into battle."

"Aren't you a dear thing, little Marjorie," he said, loud enough for my father to hear.

"It is young girls like you whom my men love. Wouldn't you like to take her home, lads?" he asked his men. They replied with wolf whistles and laughter.

Father struggled to the front line, where Valence was standing, and unsheathed his sword. He growled, "Hand her over, Valence, or next time we meet, I'll have your neck."

"Surrender now, or your daughter becomes a plaything for my men," Valence snarled, and I gagged at his disgusting breath.

Father looked from me, to Valence, to his lieutenant Jamie Douglas, who returned a nod.

He snarled at Valence, who handed me over into my father's arms, and when I looked back the English had retreated into the darkened woods.

Father did not speak to me as we mounted our horses and returned to the inn. When we arrived there, he simply told Elizabeth, Emmeline, Alvar, the children and I that we were to be looked after by my uncle Neil in Kildrummy, and we were to ride there right away. It seemed that Elizabeth had heard what happened, however, for though she was too ashamed to talk to me, she cast me pitying glances every few minutes.

You might think that Father would have beaten me for causing his loss in Methven, but he was far too intent on getting to Kildrummy right away and getting us safe. However, he was silent for the entire journey and rode fast with a murderous gaze. Everyone avoided him, even Elizabeth.

Once we reached Kildrummy, my father asked Uncle Neil for horses, and he took Elizabeth's mare and the bishop's three stallions. I had to beg him not to take Ciaran, as I could not bear being without him. Father let me keep him, but instead he had to take my mare, Isabella. Uncle Neil vowed to not let me out of his sight.

Father then left with the bishop. I do not know where, for he never told me, nor Elizabeth. It was just too dangerous to risk.

Marjorie Bruce

24th of June, 1306

During my stay here in Kildrummy, I have learnt the slightest bit of Latin. Not much, however. *Ave* is supposed to mean hail, and I just thought that I might be able to share that with you. Uncle Neil has been teaching me the ways of the world. He has taught me Latin, and he has taught me much history. And before, I thought I had all the knowledge in existence!

Elizabeth has resolved her conflict with me. I dare say that my presence was awkward at first, but her wrath had softened and I am eager to strike up conversation again. We haven't had a hearty chat since we left Ayrshire. Old Ayrshire, I miss my home. One thing Elizabeth and I have both talked about is the prospect of going back to Turnberry Castle. The outlook seems dim, as many families are being forced from their homes due to the invading English.

I have been on a few rides with Uncle Neil, and he has taken me hunting, but he has never broken his promise to Father. I have never left his sight except for when I am asleep. We hunt wild boar and deer, and while I spear the poor creature, Uncle Neil dismounts his horse and finishes the job.

Late one night, Sir Archibald Douglas, a friend of my uncle's, came to stay at Kildrummy. He had arrived in the dead of the night, when the castle was fast asleep.We were all situated around the bench in the hall the next morning to break our fast. I knew that I was eager to eat, as my stomach had been rumbling to no end the previous night. It was common courtesy, however, to wait for the guest of the house to make his appearance before commencing the meal.

A sharp slam of a door suddenly echoed throughout the house, and the tall, lean figure of Sir Archibald emerged from the dark corridor. Striding swiftly into the great hall, he smiled pleasantly and picked up his kilt to take his place at the bench across from me.

His black hair was feathery, like the down of a duck. It did not seem to be dirty at all, which caused me to begin feeling aware of my current appearance. His large brown eyes were almost invisible due to the mess of hair atop his head; it hung down in a sort of fringe. The man was of noble status, but he did not appear to be old at all. In fact, I dare say that he did not appear to be older than the age of five and twenty. There was no paunch to bring his liver to ruin, and his porcelain skin showed no sign of a beard.

"Welcome, Sir Archibald," Uncle Neil announced, standing from his seat. We followed suit and stood as well. "Ye are an invited guest of Kildrummy, and we look forward tae having ye in our company."

"I thank ye for yer hospitality," Sir Archibald replied, his voice echoing. "I shall nae outstay me welcome and I will be taking me leave in one month. May I have the pleasure of knowing who I am breaking me fast with this morn?"

He looked quizzically at Elizabeth and then at myself. Uncle Neil left his seat and walked around to where Elizabeth and I stood. "Sir Archibald, I have the great pleasure of introducing ye tae the queen of Scotland, Elizabeth de Burgh, and me brother Robert's daughter, Marjorie, princess of Scotland."

Sir Archibald leaned forward in a gracious bow immediately. Elizabeth smiled and offered the man her hand, which he kissed. I followed Elizabeth in her actions by offering Sir Archibald my hand, on which he also left a kiss.

He turned to me, saying, "Well then, Yer Royal Highness," and then he turned to Elizabeth. "Yer Majesty. It does me such a great honour tae meet ye."

Elizabeth smiled and took his hand in hers. "I return your greeting, Sir Archibald. How marvellous it is to meet one of my husband's most loyal subjects."

"Aye." He nodded and ran a hand through his long hair. "I sure try me hardest tae please the king. He shall always have me loyalty and the loyalty of the Douglas clan behind him."

His family name sounded familiar. I remembered a soldier by the last name of Douglas, but there was a chance that these two men were not of any relation at all. Still, Jamie was not unlike the man standing before me.

"Sir Archibald, are ye of any relation tae the king's right-hand man, Jamie Douglas?" I asked, remembering the soldier.

Sir Archibald grinned, his smile almost reaching to the edges of his face. "Aye, 'tis true. Jamie is me brother."

Archibald and I became fast friends. With the blessing of Uncle Neil, he accompanied me into the woods frequently for rides. We rode and rode until our horses could not carry us anymore and then spent hours on the hunt for game.

Archibald insisted that I should learn the skills of a warrior. It surprised me that he had even mentioned this idea due to the obvious fact that I am a female and thus surely do not belong in a war band. But still, I said yes. So as the morning commenced, Archie had met me in the woods by the castle where he had made a target out of a tree. Leaning against that tree was a beautiful war bow, exactly how one would have dreamt it to be. I ran towards the sleek figure and picked it up. It was light, and I felt like it belonged to me, although I had yet to learn how to use it.

Ever since I set foot on that battlefield in Methven, I had known that my destiny was not to sit behind the spinning wheel, or to embroider and bear children. I was to be a warrior, and nothing would stop me.

When Valence had held the sword to my throat, I was not worrying about death. I was looking at the men at the back of the English army—the archers. Oh, how I had longed to be an archer and feel the thrum of the cord as I loosed goose-feathered arrows. To run my hands over the sleek, smooth war bow and to slaughter an English foe with a six-foot giant. How my hatred grew for the Tyrant every day!

Archibald had told me that the bow was mine, but at the same time, it wasn't. To acquire a bow, I would have to trust it and bond with it. He demonstrated to me the power of such a thing. One attribute you needed to be an archer was strength; the others were patience and time. He told me that you could not become an archer in a matter of weeks. It took years to become a trainee, let alone a master of the art.

I watched as Archibald plucked an arrow out of his quiver and placed it on the nocking point. With precision, he eyed the target and drew the cord back to his ear, as loosing from that distance would apply more force to the arrow. Once he had targeted his aiming point, he took a deep breath and released.

The arrow flew through the air like a *fugol*, a bird. It landed with a thud in the middle of the target. It was mesmerising, beautiful even. Archibald then let me try my hand, telling me to get used to the feel of the bow in my hands. It would take time to achieve perfection, but what better time to start than now?

I stood with my feet apart, glancing at Archibald every few seconds to see whether I was correct. I held the massive bow up and changed it around a few times, just so I could get used to the weight. I took an arrow out of the quiver on my back and delicately placed it on the nocking point. I looked at the target, but I had no idea what I was doing, and so I pulled back the bowstring to test its feel. I could not pull the string back to my ear so I only pulled it back so it reached my mouth, and released. It flew for a couple feet, past the target, and landed in the shrub behind. Archibald smiled and told me to continue with practise until the sun sets and that if I wanted to become a professional, I had to practise every day.

Marjorie Bruce

1st of July, 1306

My Latin lessons have been progressing well. Uncle Neil has also been teaching me advanced French as well as Latin. After studying with Uncle Neil, I have been out and about everywhere.

Uncle Neil has finally let me go out of his sight but only for a few hours every day. I take those hours to ride Ciaran in the woods and out of town. Every time I do leave Kildrummy, I take off towards a little town called Milltown, which is a few miles south of Kildrummy. On Ciaran, it is only around a half a day's ride there and back.

I have taught Ciaran to canter, and when he has enough energy, he gallops, and gallops, and gallops. Once he starts, he will never stop. We walk out of Kildrummy together, and then, once I know that we are safe, I jump onto Ciaran and he takes me into the woods. He has to watch his step because there could be trenches or pits, and if he fell into one of those, his legs would snap.

I always ride barefoot with Ciaran, and I owe my life to my dear stallion. He saved me from a python when I was a bairn by trampling it, and with no other animal do I have such a bond.

On a long day, such as Saturday, I am able to ride to Milltown. On Sunday, the Holy Lord's day, I have less time to ride due to Mass and church services. Ciaran and I set off in the morning, and by midday we are back in Kildrummy.

On the days when I don't have as much time to ride, Ciaran and I go into the woods to hunt. I take my war bow, *Fæger*, my small quiver, and a dozen arrows. My aim has improved miraculously, and I am actually hitting the target. I haven't yet gotten used to moving targets, but practise will cure that.

You might believe that I am hysterical, but I believe that if an arrow wants to succeed on its journey, it must be blessed. So before I loose an arrow, I kiss its tip, give it my blessing, and call out its name: *Ætfleogan, Fæger!*

It translates to "fly away, beautiful."

Usually I kill at least three deer every few days, but before I let loose on them, I make sure that they are adults and that they had spent their time on Earth generously. I either take them home to Uncle Neil or ride to Milltown to sell their meat. I have made a reputation in Milltown for my sales, and I have also made a lot of money from the rich citizens of the town. Everyone wants to buy from me, and everyone in the area knows of me.

Every night, as I say prayers, I thank the Lord for the luck that he has given me with *Fæger* and with Ciaran. I am truly blessed.

Marjorie Bruce

27th of July, 1306

It has been the most tiring morning, with all my hunting and my classes, and Archibald has said I had proved to be mastering the skill of archery. I hope that my career in archery will go far, and hopefully I will lead a war band against the English.

Archibald has tested me with a new skill. He wants me to try to hunt while on horseback. Archibald says it will push me to the limits, but it will turn me into a great leader. I have told him of my ambition to lead a Scottish war band, and instead of scoffing at the idea and turning it down, he nodded. Archibald, being an archer himself, told me that if I wanted to be in the front line of a battle, I would have to wield both sword and bow.

My schedule is almost full, with archery in the mornings and sword training in the evenings. Supper is then served, and once I have finished, I am to practise battle tactics with Archibald. That only leaves Saturday and the holy day for riding and hunting.

There is an old tale that I have been told many a time by my father, who had in turn been told this story by his mother. The tale had been passed down through generations of Scots, and if I am to document it before it evaded my mind, the time is now.

In around 1333 B.C., there was a princess of Egypt by the name of Meriataten. When a rebellion started against her father, Pharaoh Akenhaten, the princess fled to Scotland where she changed her name so she could not be hunted down. She renamed herself Scota, and legend says that Scota was how Scotland got her name.

While she lived in Scotland, her husband, Milesius, is said to have forged a coin in her name to remind her of him after his death. It was a brass coin that depicted the boat Scota sailed to Scotland on and the stone that she bought with her. The same very stone was and is used for coronations of Scottish monarchs.

The brass coin, however, fell into the hands of her son Heremon, and to his son Ethriel. Seven generations had passed until Ethriel's descendant, Rothechtaid, found it in his tomb. They could not afford to lose the coin again; it was their only evidence of any link to Scota. When the time had come, Rothechtaid passed it to his loyal grandson, Sirna, as he lay on his deathbed. Sirna promised to keep it safe, but the promise was soon broken.

On a crusade through Ayrshire, Sirna carelessly dropped the coin into a small river, and the guilt for losing it on that day affected his life for years to come.

Sirna's soul was laid to rest when Marjorie of Carrick found it floating in the water of the river. She spent no time fussing over it and immediately gave it to her husband, Robert de Brus.

Robert de Brus was my grandfather, and before he died in 1304, he gave it to me, to wear and to be proud of. After I had showed it to the bishop, he had told me about the lost coin of Scota and the legacy that went with it.

Legend has it that the reason Scota gave the coin to Heremon and not to his brothers was because he had truly helped her in life and that he was the only one who believed in her. The main idea is that when you find someone who truly believes in you, someone who has helped you into becoming the person that you are, you give it to them.

I have found my person who truly believes in me: Archibald. It was a Holy Day, so I decided to approach him after Mass. I told him the story, and I told it with pride. Afterwards, Archibald seemed truly happy that I had given him this coin, although a glazed look in his eyes masked any other thought that may have wanted to escape.

Marjorie Bruce

20th of August, 1306

Yesterday Elizabeth received a letter from Aunt Christina and Aunt Mary. By the tone of the letter, it seemed that they needed to take refuge from the English as well. The Tyrant was marching again. They were storming castles and besieging villages near the lands that belonged to my aunts, and it was a wonder that no one had yet been taken hostage.

According to their letter, they are set to arrive tomorrow. They had told us that their horse-drawn litters would start trickling in the gates of Kildrummy at about noon, after Mass.

Yesterday was another full day of training, and I have successfully released 40 arrows from horseback and onto a target. Archibald says that if I am to become a feared leader, I will have to loose over 4,000 in battle. He also thanked me for the coin, and I noticed a small smile creep up the side of his face while doing so.

Archibald taught me to how to train my horse for battle. The canter is mainly used in the first charge of the battle, where the cavalry and archers spring their attack. Ciaran and I spent all morning perfecting it, after which I had to improve on my sword skills.

Like my bow, I had to bond with the sword and name it. *Crà*. Blood oath.

I fought with Archibald in the courtyard and mutilated the straw dummies he had made especially for me. He educated me in the ways of fighting and jousting and discovered my strong and weak points.

After a supper of roast deer, Archibald took me to his quarters to teach me about battle tactics. He told me that the best way to win any battle is with the element of surprise, whether it is mere trickery or an ambush.

He taught me about the way William Wallace fought. He had assembled many wooden spears and had hid them behind the army. When the English made their first cavalry charge, the Scottish army waited until the very last moment to pick up their spears. The English horses weren't ready for that sudden change and impaled themselves. From my previous knowledge, I added that having trenches dug into the ground also snaps the horse's legs and many men fall and die under the horses.

A perfectly timed ambush, Archibald mentioned, is an extraordinary surprise for the other army. They would not be ready for battle and would most plausibly be in their tents, drinking their hearts out. Their weapons wouldn't be sharpened, the armour wouldn't be ready, and the men would be caught with their breeches down, so to speak.

For some people, such as the bishop, their opinion on war is difficult to reconcile with their faith. War is a common occurrence, yet the Lord simply said, "Thou shalt not kill." Moreover, you then have the men who claim to be killing in the name of the Lord, which once again is difficult to explain. Almost everyone dies in the end, and so wouldn't every man who killed be damned?

I seem to find my faith confusing at this moment in time. It does not falter, however. It never falters.

Marjorie Bruce

21ˢᵗ of August, 1306

The day that my aunts arrived was the day that my life changed forever.

There was no training in the morning due to it being the Holy Day and because of the arrival of our visitors. Uncle Neil told me that I should welcome his sisters warmly and affectionately, though I had never met them before.

I had spent all morning in the kitchen gutting and chopping the pheasant and fish for the main meal. The dish I was to make was a beautiful, traditional meal, and any who disliked it would be daft.

In yesterday's late afternoon, Archibald had asked my permission to take Ciaran with him as he wanted to ride to Milltown after Mass. His own mare was lame and was in the process of being reshoed by Kildrummy's only blacksmith. He told me that I should stay and welcome my aunts and that he'd return in time for supper.

Through my bedroom's dirty window, I could see two horse-drawn wagons arriving at the tall gates that sheltered us from the outside world. I was anxious to see these relatives, so I moved my wooden stool closer to take a seat at the window whilst brushing my hair. The servants of the house emerged in an orderly fashion, each person attending to one carriage. By this time four more litters had arrived, these ones larger than the first two.

Once the litters had been detached from the horses that carried them, the fabric from the small carriages was pulled aside to reveal the inhabitants. I saw Emmeline step forward to assist one of my aunts, while Alvar took to the second carriage to aid my other aunt in escaping the carriage. The women that emerged were slender and tall and much like Aunt Isabel of Norway. I had only hoped that their personalities did not match.

I turned away from the window to finalise the placement of the ribbon that I had tried so hard to entwine with my hair. The time had come for me to greet them myself, so I left my bedchamber and started for the cold stairs.

Suddenly, a shrill scream shook me to my very soul. Returning urgently to my chamber, I held my hand to my rapidly beating heart as I peered once again through the dirty window. Scared footsteps crept up the stairwell and burst through the closed doors and into my room. It was the cook. Her face was flushed red as she joined me at the window, making the sign of the cross and murmuring inaudible prayers.

A gangly man held Emmeline by her long brown hair. At this moment, I was both shocked and confused at the happenings down in the courtyard. However, it did not take me long to put the cook's ramblings and Emmeline's screams together: The English were here. I opened my window and shouted her name, but it was all too late. Before she had the chance to seek the source of the scream, Aymer de Valence pulled out his sword and swiftly cut her throat. I screamed, as loud as any lady could scream. I screamed for Father, I screamed for Emmeline, and I screamed for the vengeance I would take on the English.

I wanted their blood on my hands.

Running into the weaponry room, I grabbed a short sword. It wasn't special, and it wasn't mine, but it would serve its purpose. After seeing Valence kill Emmeline, I felt numb to my core.

One guard ran inside the castle towards the area I hid in, and I tried my hardest to remember Sir Archibald's teachings. Hiding the sword behind my back, I saw him enter the weaponry room cautiously, eyes gleaming at the arrangements of weapons before him. He had then passed the place where I crouched, waiting for the right moment. The Englishman's back was turned, and sliding the sword out from under me, I thrust the sword deep into his back. Blood welled around his skin as he fell to the hard stone floor, dead. I was happy, I was free. I had murdered my first Englishman.

Archibald had always told me that you could never be sure with the English as they always seemed to have a trick up their sleeve. He had taught me that to make sure that they were dead, you would have to stab them in two places. The throat killed immediately, as did the eye. When you stabbed through the heart, the body does not fail right away, leaving time for the opponent to make one final move. If you aren't careful, it could kill you.

One Englishman dead. How many were in the vicinity of Kildrummy? I did not know.

I moved the corpse of the guard off to the side so it wouldn't raise suspicion. I had to get to the children. Alvar was nowhere to be seen. I recalled that the cook had mentioned that the children had requested to help out in the kitchens, and so I bolted downstairs. Opening the doors to the kitchen, I saw the four children sound asleep underneath one of the many tables in the room. I pitied them, as they did not yet know that their mother was dead, and Alvar most likely dead.

I silently cried as I picked up their sleeping bodies one by one and hid them in the pantry behind the bags of flour. If they were to awaken, there was no doubt that they'd be found immediately and slaughtered. I would return for them once this ordeal was over. Taking a glimpse outside, I looked back to find Aunt Christina, Aunt Mary and Elizabeth bolted up in iron cages. Later, of my own accord, I had realized what had happened.

Aunt Christina and Aunt Mary had been lodging together at an estate in Dumfries. When the Tyrant and his army marched, Dumfries had been captured, and so had the estate. The Tyrant then realized that if he wanted to capture the throne of Scotland, then he had to take something that was dear to my father. After the skirmish in Methven, Aymer de Valence had given the Tyrant an idea.

Christina and Mary were captured, and Valence had forced them to write a letter to Kildrummy, telling us to give them refuge from the English. To get through the gates of Kildrummy, Christina and Mary would have had to have been in the litters. The extra four litters were filled with Valence's men, and they had timed their attack perfectly, with an element of surprise. An ambush.

An ambush to capture the women dearest to him. Father's sisters, Elizabeth, and I.

A noise from outside drew my attention back out the window. An English archer was aiming his bow at Alvar. I smothered a cry and watched as Alvar died. I wanted to shoot an arrow from *Fæger* into that archer's eye and show him not to mess with my people. However, that would have raised suspicions as to who was fighting back. I needed to lay low.

I was glad that Ciaran and Sir Archibald were safe. I wondered whether they had sensed that something was wrong and fled to safety. This intruding thought was dismissed immediately, as my instincts told me that a good man like Sir Archibald would never do such a thing.

I told myself that when all of this was over, I was to pray for the souls of Emmeline and Alvar and everyone else who was murdered by the English.

Uncle Neil was tied to one of the cages, being tortured with a red-hot poker. I screamed as I saw the mark it left on his once-hairy chest. How it kills me to watch people in pain!

Once they had finished with Uncle Neil, I heard them speak in their Saxon tongue, not French as the high-born Englishmen did. I heard two words, "high treason," for which I, sadly, knew the punishment. Sir William had been sentenced for high treason when he was captured, and he had been hung, drawn, and quartered. Uncle Neil's face dropped when he heard his sentence, and I knew, and I believe he knew as well, that he was a dead man.

There was nothing I could do. My guardian was being hauled away before my very eyes. I felt useless as I slumped at the entrance, defeated. Uncle Neil was hauled away as I made the sign of the cross and blew him a kiss. My poor condemned uncle caught my eye and smiled, returning the kiss. I never saw him again after he was thrown into that carriage.

With tears streaming down my face, I ran to the top of the stairwell. It was hopeless, there was no one left. I had no one to run to. It was either death by the English or death by starvation, left to my own in this once familiar castle. I was going to surrender. Hearing the sound of footsteps, I stiffened. I could see Valence entering the mansion, checking the rooms for survivors. He had caused me such pain, and now he was to suffer. I wanted to send him to eternal Hell.

I hid my sword behind my back so in the case that he turned around, he would think that I was surrendering. As I edged closer towards him, I noticed that he was looking hungrily into the kitchen. A youngster's yawn made my hairs stand on end. The children were awake.

Before he could get to them, I made a commotion by stomping loudly on the steps. He turned to face me, his hungry smile growing ever so wider.

"My Lord, look what we have here. Has my dear Marjorie chosen to surrender?" he said, almost mockingly, as he walked towards me.

When he was close enough, I eyed my target down and pounced. "Not...just...yet!" I screamed as I thrust the sword from behind me into his ribcage, narrowly missing the heart. I made sure it didn't go too deep as I wanted him to keep a scar as a reminder of the pain he had caused me. Valence fell down onto his knees as I twisted the blade in his chest. He screamed in agony, and just before he fainted from blood loss, I bent down to whisper in his ear.

"That is the pain ye caused me servants, me friends, me family. I surrender to yer troops, but ken this. If ye or yer men dare tae lay one finger on me, I will vow to finish ye off for good."

And before I went outside to surrender, I stripped Aymer de Valence of his armour and kicked him hard in the place where it hurts the most.

Marjorie Bruce

Chapter Three

Excerpts from the journal of Archibald Douglas
24th of August, 1306

On returning to Kildrummy there was no one left alive. I found Emmeline, poor Emmeline slumped up against the castle wall. Her throat was slit.

Alvar was on the ground with an arrow sticking through his eye. The children were the last to be discovered. The English bastards had strung them up by their necks and hung them from a tree. But there was one noose that was unaccounted for.

I found Sorcha bleeding in the kitchen. Her arm had been severely wounded, and she was hardly alive. Sorcha had watched from the archway as her younger siblings had been killed one by one, their necks breaking as their bodies dropped from the tree. I found out later that evening that the English had not found her because she had woken up inside the pantry and had gone upstairs in search of Marjorie.

Once I had mended her arm using an old healing remedy that was used to prevent infections from occurring, I dug a pit in the courtyard of Kildrummy and gave her family a proper burial. Making the sign of the cross over the site, I said many prayers for their safe route to Heaven.

Kildrummy was a ghost town. Not one living soul remained in the once lively citadel. I needed to leave swiftly. We rode on into the night, and I kept my sword at the ready in case any English were to ambush us. Marjorie was now in the hands of Aymer de Valence, but they were not far ahead. I must have arrived only an hour or two after the town was ransacked.

The moment Marjorie gave me the brass coin of Scota, I had made a silent vow. I vowed that I would never let anything bad happen to Marjorie, and if I did, I would live with the guilt staining my soul for the rest of my life.

I knew I must follow the English to the place of Marjorie's imprisonment and set forth to set her free, even if it meant to sacrifice my own life. I would not rest until she was safe.

Archibald Douglas, Guardian of Scotland

From the journal of Marjorie Bruce
25th of August, 1306
I am in despair.

The people most dear to me are dead, and I am imprisoned. I truly do not know whether Father would be able to rescue us. If he cannot, the English will begin to make sacrifices, and I may be dead by the end of December.

The evil Valence rides with me, and I can tell that he despises me, but he is careful. It looks like he took that warning to heart, and he is right to do so.

I can't close my eyes without seeing Emmeline and Alvar in front of me, dancing with their children, and Uncle Neil lecturing me about my Latin. This was all in my head—a mere dream. They were dead and gone. I could not bring them back.

About a dozen men-at-arms also ride in my carriage. I believe this is more for the safety of Valence and less for me.

Time is passing slowly on the journey to the place of my imprisonment. I keep catching myself thinking of my late mother. Father had always said that Mother had the blondest hair in Ayrshire, as well as the longest. He always joked that she was not a real Scot because of her traditionally English looks. Her hair was said to fall in waves to her bottom, and never in her life did she cut it. I am lucky to have my mother's eyes, the palest blue you could ever imagine.

I was able to write so freely of our capture because two of the closest men in my carriage were illiterate. I could write whatever I pleased about the English bastards, and they wouldn't have been able to read it.

Elizabeth, Aunt Christina, and Aunt Mary rode in a different wagon. The upper class soldiers riding in my carriage did not pause to think whether I could understand their French tongue when chit-chatting about their recent missions. I heard from rumour that the English had orders to take all four of us women to different convents in England. I was to travel to a convent in Yorkshire, and I did not know how long it would take to get there.

It seemed that my ambition of being a Scottish archer was not possible. My dreams were shattered at the Battle of Kildrummy. *Fæger* wouldn't be of any use to me, now that I had surrendered to my captors.

One of Valence's men has just offered me a scrap of bread. I need all the strength I can get, so I took it gladly. It is growing dark outside, which indicates that I need to sleep.

Marjorie Bruce

27th of August, 1306

I was not able to write for the next two days because I had a seemingly literate soldier watch my every move. He had engaged in small conversation in the Scottish tongue with me and so naturally I assumed that he could write as well. If the soldier had caught wind of my scrawlings, the Tyrant could accuse me of treason, and I would be hung.

The rumours that I had heard were confirmed: Elizabeth and my relatives were to be distributed around England. No Scotsman would dare travel into English territory.

I am only fed in the evenings, which is a punishment for the harm I had done to Valence. Otherwise I would be fed two times a day, but I will not repent. I grow weak and lonely. The men in the wagon ignore me most of the time, and Valence won't even spare a glance in my direction.

I am still young, and I haven't aged much since I began writing in this journal. Yet March seems like years ago. I was so innocent. I hadn't the warm blood of Englishmen on my hands.

I wonder tirelessly where Archibald has gone because he surely had made it back to Kildrummy. Maybe he had left to join Father in the army. How I wish that Father had taken me with him.

It is ever so boring in the carriage, with nothing to do but review my old entries that I had written. I read the first entry I had ever written to you on the 24th of March, two days before Father was crowned. It was also at least a month before my life turned upside down. I had life so easy back home, I had nothing to worry about, and I lived free. Now I live in a wagon, surrounded by enemies taking me to God knows where.

I have been travelling for over half a week, and I strongly believe that we have almost passed the border between England and Scotland.

Oh heavenly Father, what ill fate has befallen me?

Marjorie Bruce

Extracts from the journal of Archibald Douglas
27th of August, 1306

I woke this morning to see Sorcha washing her face in the river nearby. She looked so angelic, but I knew that she was broken inside. Sorcha asked me whether Alvar, Emmeline, and her siblings were in Heaven, and of course, I told her that they were.

I miss dear Marjorie every day, as she was like a daughter to me. I had lost my own at a young age, and I had lost my wife with it. I could not bear to lose Marjorie, too.

From rumours I heard immediately after the attack, I discovered that the English were planning to take Marjorie to a convent in Yorkshire. For my sake, this bodes ill for any plan to rescue her.

If I were to rescue Marjorie, I would have to travel into England where I could be captured at any time. I would then have to break into the convent somehow and escape with the princess. With the English army alerted to our absence about an hour after our escape, we would have to ride hard and fast to get back across the border to safety. We couldn't go back to Kildrummy or Ayshire—it was too dangerous.

After much thought, I had decided that Marjorie and I were to travel to Methven. It was dead and safe. If there were any people there who could run to the English army with news of our whereabouts, they would soon have a blessed arrow in their head.

By the time I reached this decision, Sorcha was asleep. If I was to continue my journey, I had no choice but to wake her. The English wagons were falling out of my sight, and we would have to continue on if I had any hopes of following them.

We must continue on our way, for Sorcha and I have many more weary miles to travel.

Archibald Douglas, Guardian of Scotland

28th of August, 1306

I have crossed the border of Scotland with great caution.

Sorcha and I had proceeded to travel, but I was very wary of the circumstances. Only yesterday, a few hours after night fell, I had drawn my longsword and set off for an English tavern down the street.

Many English soldiers would be in there for reasons greater than the ale it served. It is where they go to celebrate whether it was a military victory, or a personal one. I made sure that I could not be seen as I crept around to the back of the thatched building.

It stunk. Of Englishmen. Of the stuff that came out of Englishmen, both ways.

The walls were covered with remains of past meals, and the floor was drowned in crap. If I was to save Marjorie, I would have to brave the stench and wait quietly. I waded into the mess and crouched down behind what looked like a rotting dog. I could not tell what anything was in the darkness that engulfed me.

My perfect moment came when a soldier, who looked about eighteen, came outside to urinate. I stayed in the shadows, waiting for the perfect moment to strike. It seemed as if he was unarmed, which was always a good sign.

Once his breeches were down, I let him have his relief and then began to make my move. I made sure that my face was hidden, so he wouldn't be able to identify me to the army, and then I jumped.

The man was shocked at my sudden appearance, to say the least, and he tried to scream. I only shoved the sword at him harder. He held up his hands in surrender before trying to pull up his breeches.

Trying to hide my accent, I motioned for him to strip. He did as he was told, and by the time he was stark naked, I was fully dressed in an English uniform. I told him to not say a word to anyone and if he did, I would make sure to revisit him in the future. The naked man ran back inside the tavern, trying to cover himself up with his hands.

I heard an uproar of laughter, a drunken retort followed by a lot more hearty laughter. I smiled and then ran back to Ciaran, who was tied up in the woods nearby.

Sorcha was waiting patiently on Ciaran as he grazed the grass that grew between the trees. When she saw me, she thought that I was an Englishman, and she screamed. When I explained that it was only me, she calmed down.

We rode through the night and through the early morning. By the time we were miles and miles away from that village, I was extremely tired. We settled down for a nap in a clearing just off of the main road.

Sorcha and I were lucky that we weren't attacked by bandits, as they were infamous for raiding and sacking around these parts. We slept for at least four hours before eating and setting off for Yorkshire.

We had been running out of supplies lately, so as I still wore the English uniform, I was able to ride to the nearest city to acquire more food. I hid Sorcha in the nearest scrub clearing under a growth of trees. Sighting a bunch of berries dangling from a branch above me, I decided that they could come in handy and eagerly picked as many as I could before telling Sorcha to stay put and not make a sound.

I rode off to the nearest English town on Ciaran, and I rode fast. Because of the raging war that Edward had created, towns were forced to lock their gates after curfew, and that curfew was nearing quickly. Citizens were always wary of strangers, and this period of time gave them no excuse to lay aside their worries. As I approached the steel gates, which held inside them a citadel rejoicing in English victory, I felt a pang of anger stab me like a thousand knives.

I thought furiously: *They do not know pain! There are families in Scotland who are dying at the hands of Englishmen, dying mercilessly! Who deserves this?*

What has Scotland done to deserve this? We were living in happiness and peace before Edward came along and ruined our lives and stained our country with blood.

England will pay, and I will be the one to issue the revenge.

"Blood will run red, my dear Marjorie and you shall help me to succeed," I said to myself, smirking at the idea of Englishmen dying. This is what I needed: motivation.

I found the berries from earlier and gripped them tightly in my hand until they popped. I smeared the juice onto my face so it created the illusion that I had an open wound. As I neared the citadel, two figures motioned for me to stop a few paces away from the gate. They were coming for inspection.

I let out a groan, hopefully giving the guards the impression that I had been attacked. I lurched forward on Ciaran, swaying in hope that the stupid fools would fall for it. They eyed me suspiciously, the bigger one holding onto his sheath just in case.

"What brings you here?" the shorter one demanded gruffly in his French tongue. He would have to know the language of the nobility, for none of the latter knew the rough Saxon tongue. I looked from him to the woodlands, contemplating my response to make sure it sounded accurate.

"I was...ambushed, my lord," I replied in the French tongue.

"Whose garrison were you positioned in, soldier?" the elder man barked.

I tried desperately to search for a name, any name, that may command an English garrison, when I remembered a particular conversation with Marjorie.

The men wanted my answer. I could feel their hunger; they suspected I was a traitor, and I had to prove them wrong.

"Valence…I was with Valence, my lord," I said, rolling the name off of my tongue with hunger for revenge. It tasted so sweet.

"I was accompanying the wagons that held the girl. I stopped to refill my canteen by a spring. The wagons carried on, and I eventually got lost. I have been searching everywhere for Sir Aymer and my garrison, but they are nowhere to be seen. Rumour has it that she is to be taken to Yorkshire, if I am correct?"

"Yes, you are quite correct. This is Yorkshire, and she is to be transported to the convent of Watton tomorrow morning, which is just at the end of those woods. May I ask how you acquired that nasty scar?" the less fearsome one asked, and then hesitated. "Or am I intruding into personal waters?"

"No, of course not, my lord. I would be delighted to tell you. About a thousand leagues away from Kildrummy there is this town, Milltown, it is so named. Apparently the girl is quite a legend in their eyes, and they were angered at the news of her capture. I was hunting for deer in the woods nearby when a group of men surprised me. Without any time to draw my sword, I was immediately surrounded and held at swordpoint.

"At first I had believed that they were English bandits, but after they started talking I recognised their Scottish tongue and from the crest on their swords, I concluded that they were to take revenge on me for the capture of the girl.

"I only had my sword and my training to defend myself. They thought I was weak, they thought that I was unarmed. And oh, were they so wrong.

"In a moment, I unsheathed my sword and swung it at the nearest Scotsman, who was caught by surprise as his head slid off of his shoulders. Perhaps I was so caught up in the moment that I did not see another sneak up behind me. I swung at another two men who smirked as they fell. To stop them from smirking, because they were really getting at me, I stabbed them through the eye and stood back as the jelly squirted upwards.

"It was then that I realised what they were smirking at as I was grabbed from behind. He pulled out a gutting knife and drew it across my face. I could feel the blood trickle down my face and it burned, it burned like nothing else you've ever felt. But before he could kill me, I threw my fist into his face and winced in pain as it shattered my knuckles, but it felled the man. With blood pouring down my cheek, or what used to be my cheek, I slit the dead man's throat and left them for the dogs, my lord."

"You've had a rough journey, I see, but how, pray tell, did your knuckles heal in such a short amount of time?" the elder asked eagerly, obviously wanting more of my lies.

"Ah, I thought you might wonder, my lord. The answer is simple. I stopped in one of the English towns along the border and called for a physician. I was taken to an elderly man who treated both my wound and my knuckles. He operated and placed a splint inside me to help regain the strength of my knuckles and gave me a bag of berries to rub on the wound. I believe it helps with the healing. This appointment with the physician was no more than a week ago, and it has really helped my health."

"Very well then, you may rest here for a few days," the elder guard informed me. "There is a tavern down the road where you are welcome to stay, and if you should need to renew supplies, our town physician will be able to aid you. He dwells in the house next to the tavern. It has been nice chatting with you, lad."

"You too, my lord," I said with a smile on my face as I waved the guards goodbye and rode into the stinking town.

Night is falling and I must sleep.

Archibald Douglas, Guardian of Scotland

30th of August, 1306

After entering the citadel, I had only a few hours before young Sorcha would starve to death and so I had to find food, fast.

A nearby tavern would most certainly have the items to replenish my stock, so I set off with Marjorie's black stallion, Ciaran, into the sound of laughter and happiness.

In the barn underneath the tavern, I tethered Ciaran to a wooden beam with a piece of hemp rope that I'd seen lying on the floor covered in horse muck. I swore disgustedly at the sight of my dirty shoes and made my way into the tavern.

It was filled with hundreds of men, some old but many young. A few times I trod on the robes of Englishmen, and many turned to give me dirty looks.

Women walked around to tables trying to seduce the men. It was a sickening business, prostitution, and many women did it just to survive. I myself had always been opposed to it because I still counted myself as married.

I seated myself at a small table as if trying to discourage English company from joining me. The stench of this place was unbearable, and drunken men were retching everywhere. I had to be wary of my enemies because they were surrounding me left, right, and centre.

A big, burly bartender pushed his way through the crowd towards me, and I thought that he had noticed that I was a Scotsman, but it turned out that he was too thick-headed for such a thing.

"What d'ya want, boy?" he growled, eyeing me up and down.

"A dozen loaves of bread and a pint of ale, my lord, if you wouldn't mind," I replied, taking caution not to anger this brute of a man.

"It'll be on its way, boy." And he said nothing more as he walked back to the bar and disappeared behind the counter.

I spent the next five minutes in observation. It seemed like the English were no different to the Scottish, except for a few kilts and thick accents that separated us. Englishmen mocked us Scotsmen for our kilts, calling us "girls" and "wee lassies." I eavesdropped on English conversation and heard many a tale of how the Scottish ran like cowards at the Battle of Methven, but I had to keep my temper, otherwise my identity would be revealed.

The bartender returned with my request, and I made for the door as soon as he had put it down on my table. Before I could set a foot outside the door, the bartender stopped me.

"Surely you can't leave just yet, boy, you haven't even finished your ale!"

"No, my lord, I was just going to bind these loaves to my horse," I replied with eagerness.

"Ah, I see. When you return, make sure you enjoy yourself here." He winked at me and then flipped me a coin as if to say, "You know what I mean."

"Thank you, sir, for your generosity," I said and then headed out the door.

It was pitch black outside, but the wind had subsided and made way for the heat. The wooden steps creaked with every move I made and I winced at how loud the sound was. It would give me away for sure.

Ciaran was still tethered onto the beam, and he didn't seem to have been troubled. The poor stallion must've been starving, though, so I gave him half a loaf of bread and a bucket of water.

" 'Tis a beautiful night, isn't it?" The voice startled me and forced me to turn to the sound.

"Hello, is anyone there?" I replied, feigning my French tongue.

"Oh, stop pretending that you are an Englishman, Douglas," the voice whispered again, taunting me.

"Who are you, and what do you want? If you don't come out from hiding, I will slice the head off of your shoulders!" I yelled into the darkness, just in time to see a figure appear from behind a white mare.

"Alexander is my name," the figure said in his thick Scottish tongue.

"Alexander who, pray tell?" I replied, eyeing this dodgy figure.

"Alex Douglas, cousin. I am here to aid you on your journey for the rightful princess of Scotland." He beamed just as I started to make out his appearance.

"How do I tell that you are not a fake, Alexander?" I inquired, drawing my sword in case he indeed was a fake.

"Your father's nephew is standing right in front of you, yet you hold him at swordpoint and do not welcome him as family. May I ask how you were brought up, dear cousin?" he retorted, with a bit of laughter in his voice and twinkle in his eyes.

"I am deeply sorry for my rudeness, cousin, but I had to make sure. There is one question that is bugging me, though, and that is, why? Why did you follow me? Why do you want to help me?" I replied.

"Well, shall we go inside and talk there? I can answer most of your questions for sure," he asked with a smile, and I immediately felt that I could trust him. So inside we went, and the bartender smiled when he saw that I had returned with another customer.

I sat Alexander down at the table that I had previously sat at, and I motioned the bartender over.

"What'll it be, boys?" he asked, this time with a smile on his face.

"Four pints, my lord." I answered for Alexander. The bartender beamed at me and then flicked a coin at Alexander.

"For your enjoyment, boys." He winked before leaving us to talk.

In the light, I could now make out Alexander's features very clearly. He was quite tall, with black, curly hair down to his shoulders. He wasn't lean or stout, and his beard was very well looked after. He looked just like a prince although he was dressed in peasant's clothes.

His deep, brown eyes had the feeling that you were being swallowed by them and that you could not escape. I must say, I also saw a lot of truth in those eyes, which made me inclined to trust him.

"Your questions...? Archie..?" He startled me again with the pet name, and I realized that I must've been so absorbed in observation that I didn't hear what he had said.

"Oh, aye. My question was, why?" I said with a small smile, just at the moment when the bartender returned with our ale.

"Thank you!" I nodded to the bartender, returning my attention to Alexander.

"Well, firstly, cousin, in my youth, I had heard a lot about you, yet I never had the chance to meet you or your brother, Jamie. When both of our fathers died at sea, I had nowhere to go, no refuge, and I believe yourself and Jamie took refuge under the arms of the king. No one would have me, I was excommunicated from the church, and I had no other family to go to. You are my only family, and whatever it takes, I should wish to seek acceptance from you, cousin."

He nodded, before adding a few more words quietly to himself.

"As you know, I am on a quest to save the girl and if you should wish to accompany me, I shall be delighted. You must know that this task is not for the faint-hearted and you should need to bring your own supplies," I replied.

"Aye, cousin. I have my mare outside with supplies for weeks yet. When shall we leave?"

"Before light tomorrow. We need to get out before we are spotted and killed. I have a young lass on this journey as well. May I ask you the favour of riding with her?"

"Aye." Alexander said nothing more after that, for the sight of a young girl stopped him.

"Hello, boys," she said with a smirk as she approached our table.

"Good evening, ma'am," I replied politely, only to hear the giggle of her friends across the other end of the room.

She placed herself onto our table, positioning herself so we couldn't get to our ale. Her beautiful, fiery red ringlets emphasised her personality; she was not one to give up.

And I was not going to give in. She tried to caress my face, but I placed my hand on hers and put it back on the table.

"I'm not interested," I mumbled.

She let out a cackle of laughter. "What did you say, boy? Did you refuse me?"

"I'm not interested," I said again, louder this time.

She smirked. "Seems like this boy is a coward. Maybe I'll just take his handsome friend here," she said as she moved towards Alex.

Alex winked at me. "I won't be long, twenty minutes at the most, cousin. Promise."

"Aye," I said with a smile. "Make sure you meet me by the barn. I'll get the horses saddled and ready."

"Have fun," I added cheekily.

Time passed and soon it was dawn. The sun was almost about to rise, and the guards were about to open the gates. Alex had met me under the tavern at the set time, and we'd saddled our horses, obtained another stallion, replenished our stock, and become sober once again. Luckily I had acquired another suit of armour for Alex from a drunken soldier who'd come to think that I was his friend. I laughed at the thought of that man rolling around on the floor drunkenly with a bleeding gut.

We were both dressed in our armour, so we set off towards the gates where we would make our escape to find Sorcha.

The same guards that had approached me the night before stopped us before leaving as well. The elder one now looked much more tired than the younger, as if they'd had a very restless night.

"Did you acquire what you had needed, soldiers?" the younger asked, before stifling a yawn.

"We sure did, my lords. My cousin and I shall trouble you no more, as we plan to leave early this morn," Alex said for me, saying exactly what I was thinking.

"You know, I never caught your names, soldiers." the eldest asked, with a large grin on his face.

"I'm Archibald, and this is Alexander, my lords," I replied with a sheepish smile.

"Archibald and Alexander who, pray tell?" the elder asked.

Alex and I exchanged glances, and I knew that we were thinking the exact same thing. A devilish smile came upon us, and we drew out our swords.

"DOUGLAS!" we yelled in our thick Scottish tongue, and I revelled in the horror that came over their faces as we beheaded them both. Our swords were wet with English blood, and I could tell that Alex was already enjoying this life as a soldier.

We looked down at the headless soldiers and smirked before we rode off into the woodlands.

Chapter Four

From the journal of Marjorie Bruce

1st of September, 1306

After weeks and weeks of travelling across the country, we finally made it to the convent that is supposed to imprison me.

It had been a dreary morning, and all I could see was trees after trees after trees. I longed for someone to come and get me. I missed Father, I missed Archibald, I missed Ciaran, and I missed Elizabeth.

Some time ago, Valence had been called away from my carriage and was replaced with a man who seemed much worse than him. His striking features showed evidence of the weariness of age and his battle-hardened soul. There was no point in arguing; if I said one word out of line, I would most likely receive his hand across my face.

I never learnt his name, so I would only know him as "The Man," and those words would frighten me for years to come.

When we stopped at the convent, a wave of relief came over me because I knew that The Man was not going to be able to access me at all times. I was safe. Well, not really, but it would do for now.

Englishmen arrived at the carriage door, and before I could get out properly, The Man pushed me over. With no one willing to catch me, I fell flat on my face.

"Get up, girl." He yelled at me, before pulling my hair so hard that it almost ripped from my skull. I got up and held my head down so he couldn't tell that I was upset.

Whatever ye do, do not let your enemy see that ye are upset. It only lets them know that they have succeeded, dear Marjorie.

Father's voice rang through my memory as I walked onward towards the convent. I didn't get far before The Man pushed me once again, taunting me, shoving dirt in my face, and I could not stand it anymore.

I yelled back at him, but as soon as I did, I regretted it. He slapped me hard across the face, then winded me by kicking me in the stomach with his armoured footwear. I fell to the ground, crying in pain, and he only laughed before whipping me thrice until I bled.

I cannot describe the pain that I felt, and I knew just who had ordered it: Valence. I was so angry and upset at the bastard that I could not think straight. I just wanted the pain to end. I eventually blacked out from blood loss, and when I woke, my tormentor was nowhere to be seen.

I was not in a bedroom, with maids and servants to wait on my every need, I was in a place much smaller than that. A place where it stunk of dung, urine, and vomit. I was cramped up in a dark space where I could not see past my own hand.

I felt around for something that could tell me where I was. It was not long before I had laid my hands on two cool, metal bars. It dawned upon me then that I was stuck in a cage. Perfect.

Marjorie Bruce

2nd of September, 1306

Only once a day am I ever called out of the cage. In the evening, Valence orders his men to escort me to his quarters for a meal.

I do not like going, and most nights I pretend that I am sleeping. The Man is usually the guard who watches over me, and I can tell that he enjoys watching me in pain. I have not yet recovered from the injuries that he gave me, because the English will not let a healer attend to me.

I have decided that I will not give up, I will not cry out in pain, and no matter how hard the English try to hold me, I will get my revenge. I will enjoy watching them writhe in agony.

Whenever I try to rest my eyes, even for a moment, The Man immediately reaches for his keys to my cage and lets himself in before waking me. I am beyond weary, for I have not slept for many days. He taunts me and mocks me, as if he knew about my nightmares. One day he told me that Valence had sliced the head off Father's shoulders and that it is now hanging on London Bridge, like his friend William Wallace. Father was not dead, I had that instinct, however the notion of his death tore me inside. I did not cry, I did not even shed one single tear because if I did, he would start beating me once again.

Dinner is usually a quiet meal. I do not even know if I should call it dinner. While Valence and his men feast on a buffet of boar, mutton, ale, and vegetables, I am fed what is left of the mutton and boar, which is hardly anything. I dare not complain because otherwise I will not be fed anything.

My water supply is sufficient because the guards fill my bowl up whenever it is low. This is good because if I don't keep my water levels up, I will not be able to stay strong, and I will just collapse.

When a member of the royal family becomes a hostage, all is done to keep you alive, although they do not have to keep you well. I believe the English are treating me badly to get Father's attention; they want him to surrender. They say that they will take over in peace, but Father is no fool.

If he surrenders to the English, Father will end up exactly like William Wallace. Dead. Cut up into pieces, with his head will be on display for all to mock and spit on. Scotland will be no more, and in no way would I ever let that happen.

I have to stay strong.

Marjorie Bruce

3rd of September, 1306

Early this morning a letter arrived for me.

The guard on duty was asleep when it was delivered at the door, but there was no way I could reach it. I just had to wait until the guard woke from his slumber, which didn't take long.

As soon as he saw the sealed parchment that lay at his feet, he didn't waste any time in ripping it open. I learnt from that very moment that he was illiterate, because he could not read the letter before him. It was in Latin, which I could read quite fluently.

I believe that he could not be bothered with travelling to Valence to translate the letter, and so he chucked the parchment into my cage with an annoyed look on his face. That was his first mistake.

"Do not tell anyone that I gave you this letter to read, girl. Translate it for me!" he growled.

I replied, shaking with fear, "Aye, my lord."

I unfolded the letter, smoothing my hands over the soft surface that held vital information. I could tell that it was rushed, maybe written while on horseback, but I could easily tell that Father did not write this to me. My heart sunk to the bottom of my chest. Father could not write or speak any Latin, but I could.

When I caught sight of the sender of this letter, my eyes widened, and my crushed hopes went soaring. It was Archibald.

I was going to be rescued tomorrow morn! My relief came out in a big sigh, and I was about to grin when I realized that the guard was still awaiting my answer. I cleared my throat before answering him.

"My lord, the letter is from me father. He wrote to tell me about the birth of his lieutenant's son. They named him Archibald." I told him, starting to feel queasy about my lie.

"Surely that is not all, girl. What else is said?" he demanded of me.

"My lord, the only other thing that he mentions is that he has no plans of attacking the English anytime soon and that his army is too weak to fight. An outbreak of sickness has swept over my father's army, and he is sick himself." I felt sick in the stomach even thinking of my father becoming ill, but surely this false information would give him an advantage.

"And why did he not write this in your filthy Scottish tongue?" the guard asked. "Surely he knew that if he wrote to our quarters, the letter would reach the guard and be translated anyhow."

I knew that he was not going to give up, but that I could win this battle if I kept my wits about me. "My lord, I believe that I do not know the reason," I cowered.

While he was pondering, I slid the letter behind my back, and started tearing it to pieces. I knew what it had said, and if I ripped it up, I could be sure that Archibald's plans were safe. Before I could finish tearing the parchment up, the guard began to eye me suspiciously.

"How do I know that you are not lying to me about the content, little girl?" he snapped, closing in on me.

"Because I know that if I lied to ye, then ye would torture me, my lord. I do not want to be hurt anymore, I cannot take it," I whimpered, trying my best to put on an act that was working in my favour.

"I'll take your word on it, girl, but if I find out that you have defied me, your head will join Wallace's. I'll make sure." He sneered once again before walking back to his post to resume his sleep.

I took the torn letter out from behind my back, and I could still just read what it had said.

'Hello, dear Marjorie.

This is Archibald speaking.

Tomorrow morning is when I plan to rescue you from the clutches of the English. If you should receive this letter, lie about the content to hide the plan. Be at the ready for any signs of our presence, and once you are free, run into the woods where your stallion and weapons are waiting for you.

Be safe, Marjorie.'

I smiled, knowing that I should soon be saved from Valence and The Man because Archie was here, and I absolutely trust him. Everything would soon be well.

Marjorie Bruce

Excerpts from the journal of Archibald Douglas
3rd of September, 1306

After I had sent that letter to Marjorie, I knew that Alexander and I had to take immediate action. We were half a day's ride away from Watton, and after noting the sentries that dotted all areas of the convent, we knew that this task would not be easy. The English would make sure of that.

Sorcha, Alexander, and I rested in the woods nearby. The trees were thick and numerous, so our little band would not have to worry about being spotted. We slept in the dirt, the horses tethered behind trees and Sorcha asleep on top of our possessions.

I believe that living in the wild has taken a toll on us all, but Sorcha the worst. She hardly sleeps, and when she does, it's always restless. When we have saved Marjorie, we shall all need to travel to Methven to heal from our injuries.

We only had a couple of hours' sleep. When I woke, Alexander was readying the horses for our silent journey into Watton. Ciaran was to stay here, hidden in the scrub.

I bent down to wake Sorcha when I felt Alex's hand come to rest on my shoulders.

"No, do not wake her," he said firmly.

"Alexander, she needs to come. She is only four summers, and she cannot take care of herself," I replied.

"She is four summers? 'Tis still a bairn! No, the lass must stay here where she will be hidden. If she does come, her life will most probably be ended!" Alexander hissed this time with a glint of anger in his eyes.

"Och...fine! Ye get your way!" I said before gently kissing the lass on her forehead.

Alexander smiled. "Let's hope the sound of the dying Englishmen does not wake her."

I chuckled before mounting my stallion and joining my companion at the edge of the dark wood.

"Alexander, make sure ye ride silently and cautiously. Ye are to enter the town and question townfolk about where Marjorie is. Give a false identity and name yerself as a soldier under Valence. They will let ye enter. Marjorie does not know about ye, so she might not expect ye and panic. Just make sure ye introduce yerself.

"Knock out the guards quietly as ye go along, and if they put up a fight, kill them. I will be following behind, making sure that ye are not being hunted. Once ye exit the convent, ride to where Sorcha and I will be. Marjorie will ride Ciaran, and we shall disappear."

Looking over at him, I noticed the mischievous gleam in his eye and his devilish smile. "Let us ride," I declared.

Men are going to die tonight.

Archibald Douglas, Guardian of Scotland

Excerpts from the journal of Alexander Douglas

We approached Watton ever so slowly. The convent was like a fortress, teeming with guards at every entrance.

I rode Briana, my white mare, to the entrance of the convent. My sword was sheathed, and I held my hands up in the air to show that I came in peace.

As I rode along the cobblestone road, the air thickened with the smell of food, yet I knew that Marjorie would not be sharing in that feast. Two guards noticed me as I advanced forward and unsheathed their swords.

What a pleasant welcome, I thought.

I studied the men from top to bottom, noting important information about them. The Englishman who approached me from my right was a left hander, an advantage for me. I would easily be able to fend him off.

"Name," the man on my left barked.

I thought for a moment before coming up with an English name. "Richard Abbott."

"What is your purpose here at Watton?" he asked, paying less attention to me and more to a bonny lass who sat at the end of the street.

"I was summoned by Sir Aymer de Valence, my lord. I am skilled in the profession of healing, and Sir Aymer sent for me to tend to the Scottish scum," I replied, the latter two words choking me. I had never referred to a Scottish royal as scum before, but in order to save that royal's life, I now had to.

"Right then. I'm assuming that you'll need an escort?" he offered, and I accepted, for if I didn't it would only raise their suspicions higher.

"As you wish, my lord. I predict that the girl is feasting at this moment, so the escort and I shall wait in her quarters until she arrives," I said, taking charge of the offer.

The guards just nodded and opened the gate for me, but they did not let me in until an escort was by my side.

My escort appeared to be a mere lad of fourteen who had joined the English army to help his family survive. The lad led Briana to the convent's stables whilst I noted where they were located so I could reach my mare later. The stables were surprisingly clean, most probably the handiwork of the young boy beside me. Many of the horses inside were stallions, although there were at least one or two mares. The lad tethered Briana to a wooden beam before kneeling down at my feet.

"Aaron Barclay at your service, my lord," he said, speaking for the first time in the French tongue.

"Richard Abbott at yours. Now, which way to the girl's chambers, Aaron?" I asked.

"This way, my lord. Just down the corridor and two doors down, that is her chamber," he replied, before turning away quickly.

"Aren't you going to escort me, Aaron? Or have you got something on your mind?" I asked, knowing that it was most probably a lass.

He winced. "Yes, my lord. It is my betrothed. She is expecting me at this time."

I let out a hearty laugh. "Ah, I see, Aaron. Go and find her, and if they ask where you are, I shall tell them that you have retired for this night."

"Many thanks, my lord. I shall forever be at your service," he said, a grin on his face, before he departed.

I turned to watch a blond mop of hair sprinting through the corridors. *Things are going to turn out for the better, I guess.* I checked to see whether any sentries were making their way towards me, and when I noticed that they hadn't, I ran towards Marjorie's chambers. I was still dressed as an Englishman. I realized then that this detail might make the task of befriending Marjorie even harder, given that she had never laid eyes on my person before.

Approaching the door, I peeked through the crack and saw a sentry who was alert but tired. I decided that I had to make a choice, either to get rid of the guard permanently or to remove him temporarily.

I cleared my throat before entering, my eyes falling on the small cage that held the princess of Scotland. She looked so weak and frightened. Only nine summers old she was, but so beaten and broken. She gazed at me intently, as if she were trying to figure out my whole life story. Those eyes were what had brought me close to tears.

"Excuse me. Who are you, and why are you 'ere?" the sentry demanded of me.

"Richard Abbott, my lord. Well-known physician all around England. It is by request of Sir Valence, that I must treat this, uh, pest." I grimaced and spat at the floor near Marjorie.

The hurt in her eyes bombarded me with guilt, even though I knew I was here to save her blue eyes were brimming with tears, and although she turned away, she was hurt genuinely.

My attention was turned back to the guard, who looked at me with a face full of scorn.

"Well, then, 'ow come I 'aven't heard of you?"

"Look, my lord. I do not care for the fact of your hearing of me or not. My job here is to heal this girl. I believe I may need to work near the stream at the break of the woods. The stream provides running water, which is needed for what I am to perform. Will you care to escort me?" I replied, my heart aching for Marjorie.

"I guess I could then. 'Twill only be 'alf an hour, and next sentry isn't due for a full hour. No one will notice if I'm gone. On with it, then. We 'aven't got long."

The guard smirked as he unlocked the cage. He pulled her out, and I was immediately sickened by the way he looked at her. Before he could make a move, I grabbed her hand and hauled her out into the corridor. She was weak, and if she was kept in these conditions, she wouldn't last until December.

As we wandered through the hall, I reminded myself of where Aaron had taken me to tether Briana. To get into the woods, I would need her. Marjorie trailed behind me in the clutches of the guard. Wolf whistles were heard all throughout the convent, and many men spat at her feet. I felt the anger boil up inside of me, only to realise that if I blew, it would end not only my life, but Marjorie's as well.

The barn lay before us, and as soon as Marjorie saw my mare, her eyes lightened, and she spoke for the first time.

"Will we be riding her, my lords?" she asked innocently before feeling the hand of the guard across her face. She then shied away.

We continued walking towards the barn, where we would ride out to safety, and once we got there, Marjorie immediately leapt up on Briana. She giggled and ran her hand through her mane.

"You are to leave, after you treat 'er?" the guard asked nonchalantly.

I had such an urge to respond with "aye," but I resisted it.

"Yes, my lord. I expect that you will take her back to her chambers?" I replied, turning to face him.

He hopped up onto his stallion. "Of course. Now, shall we ride?"

I only nodded, before mounting Briana and starting her into a canter.

The guards motioned for us to stop, but when they saw the guard with us, they immediately let us through. We rode across the cobblestone road until I found a clearing in the woods. This was our meeting point.

I looked back to see whether anyone was following, and when I had found that none were, we rode into the woods. I tried not to lead the Englishman anywhere near Archie and Sorcha, and when we arrived at the clearing, I could see Archie watching us from a few leagues away.

I dismounted Briana, and I helped Marjorie off. Once she landed, she gave a little curtsey. I noticed a small fire up ahead close to the banks of the river and shifted the guard's attention towards it before pushing Marjorie behind me. I unsheathed my sword quietly, the metal softly emerging with a clink as I readied myself to do battle with this man. If I didn't want men to come rushing out of the castle, I would have to make sure that his death was swift.

"So, have you ever come across a Scotsman before?" I asked casually, causing him to raise his eyebrows in suspicion.

"No, why?" he answered, before touching the hilt of his sword.

"You must wonder what they are like, then," I added, and I could see that he was getting scared.

"I know what they are like. They are filthy, rotten scum who deserve nothing more than to die!" he growled.

I unsheathed my sword and held it at his throat.

"Say that again, bastard," I growled back.

He did not say anything back but accepted that death was at his feet and whimpered.

"Do ye know who I am?"

"No, no, my lord. Please make it quick." He sobbed uncontrollably.

"I am a Douglas, one of the guardians of Scotland. Aye, I will make yer death quick, weakling." I smirked before taking a few steps back to bow to him mockingly, and then with one swipe of my sword, I slit his throat.

I turned back to Marjorie, who had mounted Briana and was now looking at me with cautious eyes. She spoke for the second time: "Archie? Ye dinnae look like him."

"Och...no, Princess. 'Tis his cousin, Alexander Douglas. Archie is waiting for ye in the woods," I replied, with a smile on my face. "Let's get ye outta here, shall we?"

"Aye, I would like that." She smiled at me, before continuing our journey over to Archie, who was waiting for us with a grin.

Alexander Douglas

Chapter Five

From the journal of His Majesty, Robert the Bruce of Scotland
18th of January, 1307

Not a day goes past without my dearest daughter and wife crossing my mind. It tortures me to know that the people that I hold closest to in my heart are hurt and no doubt at this moment being hurt.

People might give me remarks such as, "At least they're not dead," but the truth is that I am not fine without them. They are the people who make my life complete, my world whole.

I never imagined that when I became king, I would be risking not only my neck, but my whole family's necks. If I had to turn back time, I would have never left Marjorie at Kildrummy. Yes, I was angry with her at that moment, but if I had known what was to happen, I would've taken her and the others away with me. Far, far away, where they would be safe in the comfort of my army.

Emmeline, Alvar, the children—dead. Archibald Douglas—unaccounted for. Marjorie, Christina, Mary, Elizabeth—captured. My brother-in-law Christopher, my brother Neil—awaiting execution in England.

So many people were taken from my life that fateful day in Kildrummy, and I shall forever hold them dearest in my hearts.

If the English want war—they are going to get it. They will not win—they will pay; they will pay the price of murder.

My army made haste towards Ireland, where we landed not a few days past. I had only been to Ireland once in my youth, and now it was my time to call upon my friends to aid Scotland against the English.

Time to bring out your charm, Robbie, I thought to myself.

I had been warmly invited to the kingdom of Tír Eoghaín by the King Domhnall mac Brian Ò Neíll, who has been an ally of Scotland for many years. I could not think of a better person to discuss war tactics with.

The army has taken refuge with the Irish, which will give them time to bond and sort out their differences. My lieutenant, Jamie Douglas, has been given a room inside the castle and is just as welcome as I am. I believe this to be because the Douglas family has allied with Ireland for generations past.

Although I am welcome in Ireland, I also have many enemies. Enemies who still believe that John Comyn was the rightful heir to the throne. Whenever that name is spoken, it sends chills down my spine. It reminds me of the time that I smelt of ale and vomit. I sincerely did not mean to do what I did, but I shall never be the same after that day; I sinned, and the whole world knows it.

Robert Bruce, King of Scotland

20th of January, 1307

I woke up yesterday to an annoying butler who would not stop knocking at my door. I had to be down in the dining hall before noon.

Reluctantly, I let the butler in, and he helped me dress. Layer after layer of clothing went on, the tunic, the kilt, the shoes, the Bruce plaid, my chain mail, and my breastplates. I had to be wary, even in a country we are allied with.

I sheathed *Molreach*, which I have had for over forty years, ever since I was a wee bairn. It was the present from my father to my mother when they were married and for their first-born son, which was me.

I turned around to see the butler reaching to open the door for me. He seemed very frightened of me.

"Boy," I began, in my softest voice. "I believe I never got yer name."

He smiled weakly and started to talk, brushing his long, brown fringe aside.

"Colin, sire. Colin Kellis."

"Ah. May I ask ye a wee favour, Colin Kellis?" I smiled back at him.

"Anything, sire," he replied, becoming more confident with every word.

"I need to visit my army this eve, so I would like ye to polish my sword and armour when I get back. I would also love a bath, perhaps with a bar of sweet-smelling soap. Thank ye, Colin."

"Of course, sire," he said, before escorting me out the door.

The meeting had not yet commenced downstairs, and as I came to the last step that led to the dining room, I heard Colin clear his throat, causing the whole party to turn their heads to us.

I saw King Domhnall crack a smile just before he introduced me to the in-quisitive group of men.

"Ah, King Robert Bruce, I see you've come to join us," he said, gesturing us in with that unmistakable vivacious Irish spirit.

"Aye, my lord," I said while walking forward, studying the faces of all the men.

"Now, now, none of those formalities here. I am just Domhnall, not king, not sire, not my lord. Come and take a seat, and I shall introduce you. Is Jamie Dou-glas not able to join us, Robert?" he said, with a disappointed look on his face.

"I'm afraid not, Domhnall. He has been bedridden with sickness ever since we arrived in Ireland. I believe he is faring better, though," I replied, taking a seat next to the king.

"Well, that's too bad. I shall visit him once this meeting has been dismissed. Now back to business," he said, addressing the whole table.

"I welcome you all to the kingdom of Tír Eoghaín. We are here to discuss war on behalf of our allies, the Scots. As you have been informed, Scotland has been taken over by the English, and they are desperately fighting to regain the country as their own. King Robert Bruce and his lieutenant, Jamie Douglas, have called upon us, the Irish, to help the Scots win this battle. The whole Scottish army has travelled here and lost men along the way to ask us for help, and I believe that we should come together and help them," Domhnall began, obviously proud that his kingdom had been called upon.

"What's in it for us, then?" a short, bald man shouted from the rear.

Domhnall looked like he was about to speak, but I knew that I had to propose this offer myself.

"May I?" I asked hopefully.

"Carry on," the king said, smiling.

"Sir, as the king of Scotland, I propose an offer for ye and ye men," I began, sitting up straighter than before.

"If ye aid us in regaining Scotland as our own, then I can pay ye an amount of coins that we can settle on. Also, whenever ye need our army, we will gladly help, no matter how bad the trouble is. Ye are also always welcome in Scotland, and ye can walk our lands without fear of being killed. Any man who does try to kill ye will be arrested for treason and dealt with accordingly. Ye will not be refused entry from our taverns, hotels, or markets, and ye are always welcome at our castle in Ayrshire," I concluded, sitting back with a smile on my face.

"Seems fair. What about 20,000 in Scottish groats?" the Irishman suggested, rising from his seat and walking around to where I sat. "Is that a just price, my lord?"

I stood to welcome him as he shook my hand warmly.

"Aye, 'tis a reasonable amount. I thank ye greatly for ye support. Robert Bruce of Scotland, my lord," I said with a smile, knowing that I had won this man over.

"Sir Malcolm Sullivan of Ireland, my lord. Pleasure to meet you at last," he said before turning to his friends.

"Well, I say that we help the Scottish win back their freedom. And I am in." He turned back to me, kneeling down in the process. I held out my hand, and he took it in his and kissed it. I had a supporter.

The men who had once sat at the table, looking like they could really be somewhere else, pledged their allegiance to me one by one. These men had small armies of their own around Ireland who would soon be making their way to the kingdom of Tír Eoghaín.

Before each of the men left to their quarters to write missives to their armies, they bent their heads down into a bow, and exited the room. Domhnall and I were the only men in the hall.

He turned to me, smiling ecstatically.

"That sure went well! The missives shall be sent on the morrow, and the armies should arrive in a fortnight at the latest. Now, the men of nobility are joining me for dinner. I should like to invite Jamie and yourself, if he is well enough," he suggested.

"Of course, Domhnall. I shall love to join ye. I'm not so sure about Jamie, though. I shall ask him if he is up to it. Before I join ye for dinner, I need to visit my army down in the village this afternoon. I may need an escort," I stated.

"Certainly, I shall have one sent to you in an hour. Thank you for joining me, Robert."

"My pleasure," I said before walking back through the hall to the stone steps.

I was filled with relief that this task was over. I had truly thought Malcolm was going to object. No words could describe how excited I was that the Irish would be joining us for the remainder of the war.

Once I had gotten back to my room, I immediately walked into my bathing chambers, inspecting what I was to bathe in. I found my bathing tub full to the rim of ice-cold water. Exactly what I had pictured. Next to the tub were two bars of soap, one that smelt like sweet honey, and the other smelling more masculine.

I left the chamber and walked over to my bed. Reaching for a quill feather and ink pot, I wrote Colin a note and placed it on my bed. The note stated that I was in my bathing chambers and for him to commence polishing. I placed my breastplates, shoulder plates, helmet, shield, and sword on my bed next to the note.

I then began to undress, leaving all my dirty clothes on the floor for the maid to wash. Once I was naked, I began to inspect my body for any sign of illness that might need to be attended to by a healer. Fortunately, there was none to be found. I grasped the sweet-smelling soap before plunging my body into the ice water.

I winced; this was certainly cold water. I thoroughly scrubbed my face and body until I was pleased with myself. It wasn't every day that you got to bathe like this. In fact, it was hardly ever.

Seizing the more masculine-scented bar of soap, I rubbed it all through my dense red hair and beard until I could see dirt and crumbs floating in the nearly brown water around me. I was starting to doze off when a knock on the door startled me.

"Come in," I said, knowing that it was Colin.

He walked in through the chamber door, before bowing.

"My lord, your armour and weaponry are polished, your clothes are washed, and your escort will arrive in five minutes." He smiled.

"Thank ye, Colin," I said, before dismissing him.

It had been an hour that I'd spent in the tub, although it didn't feel anything like it.

I stepped out of the tub, looking back disgustedly at the dirt that had lived on my body for the past few weeks. Clutching a white cotton towel, I dried myself off before entering the room. My armour and clothing were laid neatly on my bed. Colin had even bothered to polish my family badge.

I dressed myself before using a whalebone hairbrush to comb my hair and beard. I certainly smelt and looked better.

As soon as the escort arrived, I sheathed my sword and set off for my lieutenant's quarters. It seemed that he was only rooming a couple of doors down.

Once I had arrived at the doorway, I gave a nod to the escort, who stepped away for a couple of minutes. I knocked thrice, the third time receiving an answer. It wasn't much more than a mumble of "come in."

I opened the door slowly, hoping not to disturb anyone in the next room. The door gave way to a sight which was nowhere near as pretty as I would have liked. I chuckled quietly, hoping that he wouldn't notice me.

Jamie Douglas was standing at a mirror, completely naked, surveying his body like it was an anatomical project. He brushed his curls to the side, before flexing his arms. I was almost splitting my sides with laughter.

"Towel please, Colin," he finally said, still adoring himself in the mirror.

"Who do ye think I am? Yer bloody servant?" I replied, longing for him to turn around.

He turned around, and his brown eyes widened in shock as he saw me standing there.

"ROBBIE!" he screeched, before pulling a towel off of the bed and covering himself. We both began to laugh at his embarrassment.

"How are ye, Jamie? I heard that ye are sick," I started, pulling him into an embrace.

"Aye, Rob. Nothing but a day fever, I hope. I believe to have caught it off of one of the peasants. Just had a bath, I feel much better already," he replied, giving me one of his famous toothy smiles.

"Ah, it does seem to help. Now, King Domhnall has invited us to dinner. He will be disappointed if ye don't show. As will I. At this moment, I am off to visit the men in the village. If ye want to attend tonight, I suggest ye rest for awhile, lad," I said.

"Aye, I will show. Ye can count on me, Robbie! Shall I arrive at yer quarters by half-past six?"

"That would be perfect. Have a rest now, and maybe ye can show off one of those moves tonight?" I winked at him, indicating that ladies would be present.

He laughed, before waving me off and leaping into his four-poster bed. That was my cue to leave the room.

The escort and I then began down the corridor, through the dining hall, and out into the castle's garden. Although it wasn't much of a garden, the view was spectacular. A dozen lush, rolling hills spotted the horizon, and the bustling crowd of townsfolk going about their business gave me a sense of peace and tranquillity.

We started out of the gate and followed a path down into the village. Many eyes fell on me, but no one gave me more than a curious glance in my direction. It seemed as if not many folk knew my figure, and that was a good sign.

The escort led me down an alleyway behind a shop, and then back onto another main street. A couple of houses later, we arrived at a wooden shelter well-hidden from prying eyes. Two of my men came out from the shelter to welcome me.

"David, John, I see that ye have taken a liking to this place." I smiled.

"Aye, sire. We grow to love Ireland as much as our own country, the men here are extremely friendly," David replied, with John giving a nod.

"Well, lads, it seems as if the nobility have taken a liking to me, too! They accepted the deal and have written missives to their armies, who should be here in under a fortnight," I relayed ecstatically, before continuing.

"Ask the Irishmen if they would take ye out on an expedition in the morn, perhaps to catch some wild boar. It will get ye into the fighting spirit," I suggested to them.

"Aye, sire. I shall ask, and I guess that an expedition is what we all need. To get away from a cooped-up space," David replied, happy with the suggestion that I made.

"That settles it then. Tomorrow ye hunt. Enjoy yerselves, lads," I said, before dismissing them.

They ran back into their shelter, shouting with delight. Once I was a couple of paces away, I heard an uproar of joyful shouts commence.

I would do anything to please my men.

As I kept walking into the ever-growing crowd, I felt something slam into my left side. I twisted around, ready to fight if I was to be harmed. It turned out not to be an enemy, but a small, slender lady who had run into me.

I noticed her snowy, white hair, her pale blue eyes, a pale blue dress to match, and the ring that sat on her hand. Surely with a gown like hers, and the ring that she wore, she had to be of high nobility. Something about her even looked familiar, as if I had seen a portrait of her somewhere.

"My lady, I am so terribly sorry," I said as I picked her off of the ground.

She gave me a smile that could melt hearts. "Do not worry, King Robert. It's not like Domhnall will yell at you or kick you out of the castle," she said as she winked cheekily at me.

"Lady Maeve! Oh, how nice it is to run into ye, so to speak." I chuckled at my own joke, realising that this was in fact King Domhnall's wife.

"I suspect that I will be seeing you tonight at dinner then?"

"Of course, my lady. I wouldn't miss it for the world," I answered, before taking her slender hand and touching it to my lips.

"Until next time, then?" She blushed.

"Till next time," I agreed, before once again disappearing into the crowd. *Goodness, she was a beauty.*

About an hour before dinner began, a knock on the door interrupted my peace.

"Jamie, if that is ye, I swear I will wring yer neck," I chuckled, hearing the door to my room open.

"Aye, Rob. I'm here to get ye advice on a coupla things." He winked at me.

"Such as…" I started, knowing exactly what he was meaning.

"How to charm the ladies." He grinned sheepishly.

This ought to be interesting, I thought, and I was right. After half an hour or so reminiscing on my old days of courting, Jamie and I began to make our way down to the dining hall, where a bright glow radiated from the room.

Men were dancing with their women, holding them close. Irish bagpipes were playing in the corner, and King Domhnall and Lady Maeve were seated at the round table, drinking pints of ale.

As we were invited into the room by the drunken king, Lady Maeve bowed her head towards Jamie and I, before motioning us to sit down.

"Gee, she's a looker." Jamie may have thought he was whispering to me, but his voice obviously carried, because a blush immediately appeared on Maeve's face.

I chuckled, looking at Jamie, who was observing every woman in this room.

"She's taken," I stated, as King Domhnall placed a wet kiss upon her lips.

We were then interrupted by the man I had met earlier, Malcolm, and his wife.

"Nice to see you again, sire. May I introduce my beautiful wife, Lady Bridie Sullivan," he said proudly.

The small, shy brunette blushed. She looked no more than eighteen summers, although I believed Malcolm to be almost fifty.

"'Tis a pleasure to meet you, sire," she said, as I brought her hand to my lips.

"Aye, and ye too, Lady Bridie. This is my most trusted lieutenant and friend, Sir Jamie Douglas," I said as I introduced Jamie to the couple.

"Aye, my lord and lady. 'Tis most a pleasure to meet ye. Lord Sullivan, may I say how lucky ye are to have such a bonny lass?" Jamie smiled, using his natural charm. Bridie blushed, and her cheeks turned a rosy pink.

"Thank you, Sir Jamie. It is most appreciated," Malcolm said, before introducing another couple that had begun to start towards us.

"May I introduce Lord Iain Farrelly and his new bride, Lady Caoilinn Farrelly," Malcolm stated, before Iain grabbed my hand in his and shook it thoroughly.

"It is such a pleasure, sire. I am glad to become your acquaintance." He smiled. Lady Caoilinn then did the same as I introduced her to Jamie.

We all took our places at the table while butlers served up pints of ale and plates of beef.

I was halfway through my meal when two men excused themselves and walked around to my place at the table. I turned around to see them smiling at me.

"Lord Lachlan Connaigh and Lord Niall O'Doherty at your service, sire."

I smiled back. These two men were like Jamie, unmarried and out to impress the ladies.

"Glad to make yer acquaintance, my lords. Now, shall we eat?" I suggested, and they nodded before returning to their seats.

Throughout the evening, there was one lady who did not get up once, not even for a dance. Her husband stayed by her side, as if he was a lion protecting his lioness. I decided to introduce myself, and when Jamie followed behind, a smile came upon her face.

"Sire, I am terribly sorry that I have not been more sociable. At this point in time, it is a little hard for me to walk anywhere. Lady Nessa O'Ryan, sire," she said with an expression of concern on her face.

"'Tis not a worry, Lady Nessa. I am Robert the Bruce, although ye may call me Rob. This is my dear friend and lieutenant Sir Jamie Douglas. May I ask what ails you, Lady Nessa?" I smiled back at her.

She began to stand, but as soon as she did, she began to falter. Luckily her husband supported her, and her ailment was revealed.

"Congratulations, Lord and Lady O'Ryan!" Jamie exploded. It became clear that Lady Nessa was carrying a bairn, which was always a joyous time.

Lady Nessa blushed at Jamie's outburst, and Lord O'Ryan cracked a smile.

"Lord Hector O'Ryan, sire," he said as he grasped my hand.

"Robert Bruce, my lord." I grinned, as we drank the night away.

Later that night, Jamie and I lay in my quarters, extremely drunk. His naturally curly hair had been tangled and lay in a mess on top of his head.

I couldn't think straight, and neither could Jamie. Until the morning came, we babbled on about such nonsense.

"Ye know, Robbie," Jamie began, intoxicated. "I think I'm in love with Lady Bridie…"

I waited for him to finish his sentence, but heard nothing but snoring. I chuckled drunkenly to myself, before passing out on the bed next to Jamie.

Robert Bruce, King of Scotland

Chapter Six

From the journal of Marjorie Bruce

22nd of January, 1307

The very morning that I escaped, I was introduced to Alexander Douglas. At first I was afraid that he would kill me before Archie rescued me, but it didn't take long to figure out that he was an ally.

We rode into the woods to find Archie, and when we eventually did, I embraced him in a passionate hug. Oh, how I had missed him.

Ciaran was in Archie's hands, waiting patiently for me. Two more horses lingered, and on one sat a small figure. It was Sorcha! She looked fatigued, malnourished, and most of all worried. I can't imagine what she had been through. Her mother and her siblings had all been killed before her eyes, and she narrowly escaped the clutches of death herself.

I jumped onto Ciaran, eager to ride him once again. My sword, bow, quiver, and arrows were tied up in a burlap sack to prevent the loss of them. As much as I wanted to use my bow at this moment, I knew that it wasn't possible. In just a few minutes, a sentry would find the dead guard and raise the alarm that I was missing.

Many men would be sent after me, and that is why we had to ride hard and fast into the dawn.

We had ridden for about ten miles when Archie halted up ahead. He was looking down at something that hid in the scrub. With a flick of his wrist, he motioned for us to follow him downhill, even though it held treacherous footing for the horses. We reached the end of the path safely, and Archie led us into a small wooden cottage.

Algae had stained the dank walls of the rotting house, but it still stood its ground. The door had been boarded up with nails, a positive sign that it had been abandoned. The three of us carefully dismounted our horses, not wanting to cause a commotion.

Archie peered through the glass windows to see nothing out of sorts. It looked safe. Using his sword, he pried away the nails, causing the rotting boards over the door to fall. Dust flew out into the open air, free from many years of captivity.

He gripped his sword tightly as he entered the house, in case it was a trap to lure us in. Alex followed swiftly behind, clutching my arm tightly as I was drawn into this abandoned cottage. Rays of sunlight filtered through the broken roof, shining on the green patches of moss that grew in the cracks. A table sat in the middle of the room, waiting for someone, anyone, to relieve the silence that captured this house.

Suddenly, memories flooded my head. I found myself reliving all the stories my father told me about this house and the countless times I had cried over a mere story, but this time I knew it was real.

"It looks safe," I croaked, my voice caught up in so many overwhelming memories.

"What ails ye, Marjorie? Ye look like ye are about to cry," Alex questioned, ignorant of my past and my surroundings.

Archie looked up from a piece of parchment that he had been reading. It sat on the bench, collecting dust over the nine years that it had been abandoned. He knew about it too, and I glimpsed a flash of regret cross his eyes.

"Alexander, we should give Marjorie some space. Let us explore outside," Archie said before guiding Alex and Sorcha out of the house.

When I could not see them anymore, I sat down in a wooden chair that I had been led to believe was hers. Tears filled my eyes as I scanned the rotting house. It used to be beautiful, like in the stories Father told me. A ring of the finest make sat on the table, rusting with age.

I picked it up carefully, understanding the pain she must have felt. Guilt streamed through my veins as I wept.

I did this to her! If I hadn't been saved, she would have lived. It was my fault all along!

I screamed, pain and guilt swallowing me whole as I was swept into darkness.

A woman lay on the floor, screaming in pain. Darkness was on the verge of her mind; she knew that she would not make it through the birth.

Blood stained the linen that she lay on, her maid by her side, feeding her water. A lone male sat by her, weeping with agony. He was drunk, but sober enough to realise that this would be the death of her. He loved the woman more than anything; she was his partner, his true love.

His red beard was stained with tears as he stood up from the wooden chair. He paced the room aggressively, stopping to stand in a ray of sunlight that shone through the broken roof. The male dipped a goose-feathered quill in ink before writing her will on the parchment that stood before him. He prayed for almost an hour before the screaming of his wife became unbearable.

The woman whimpered as she pushed her long, blonde hair aside, and gave the final push. The male whooped with delight as the maid presented him with his blonde-haired bairn, a wee lass.

His attention turned towards his wife, who looked like death herself. The tears started once again as he knelt beside the woman. She made a motion for him to take her wedding ring off, and as he did, he kissed it once and placed it on the table, where it would lie for many years to come, untouched.

"I love ye, husband," she whispered to him quietly.

"I love ye too, Isabell. Do not forget that." He smiled at her, before placing a kiss on her sweaty forehead.

"Give the ring to the lad who marries our bairn, Robert," she said as her eyes closed, giving her only a few seconds before she faded.

"Aye, I shall." He wept.

"I love ye, Marjorie…" she whispered before death took her.

The male huddled up to his late wife, cuddling her until she turned cold. He ran outside with his bairn, weeping with despair at the loss of his wife.

As the maid carried the woman out onto her horse, they mounted their horses and left the ruined cottage to rot, forgetting the ring in the process.

I woke hours later, still entranced by the memory that surrounds this particular house. Alex, Archie, and Sorcha were sitting at the table, the men looking concerned about my condition. I could almost understand what they were saying.

"I feel horrible now that I led her down here. I had no idea that she would know. 'Tis an awful thing to remember." Archie shifted.

"Aye. No one should have to visit the place of their mammy's death. We should leave as soon as possible," Alex suggested.

Eyeing the ring that still sat untouched on the table, Archie began to talk once again.

"I should give this to the king, and when the time comes, he shall give it to the lad who should marry the lass."

"Aye. And we shall leave this place in peace, knowing of its true story," Alex said, standing up. Clasping his hands together and kneeling on the floor, he began to pray.

"In the name of the Mother, the Holy Ghost, and the Lord above, I grant thee, Queen Isabell of Mar, a safe path to Heaven and an afterlife of frolicking in the gardens above. We know that ye are watching us at this moment, and ye shall sit with a smile on yer face as ye watch yer beautiful wee lass grow up. I promise to keep her safe. Amen."

Archie did the same as I wandered over to join them. They did not break their prayer once to even look at me.

"We should leave," I said, breaking the silence.

The two men looked up at me, tears glistening in their eyes. They said not a thing, but escorted me towards the horses.

Leaving the scrub that housed so many memories, I said my last goodbye to my mother.

May the Lord give you a safe haven, Mother.

25th of January, 1307

We had ridden for days on end, not looking back once to where we had come from. I did not want to remember anything about *that* encounter, even though it was still fresh in my mind.

We were now fugitives of the English, and both Archie and Alexander had a price on their heads. That was why we needed to escape so desperately. The four of us rode through the woods, not risking the main road, for we would surely be caught there.

We decided to rest deep in the woods for a night. After dismounting the horses and tethering them to the nearest tree, we huddled together, our weapons by our sides in case we needed them. The evening mist began to settle in, and as the night passed by, the atmosphere grew colder.

Water droplets formed on the surrounding forest leaves, granting us a drink that we hadn't had for ages. Short of supplies, we rationed every piece of food and water that we had. There was no place for mistakes.

We were cold and hungry; hypothermia was starting to set in. If we didn't heat up soon, the four of us would surely die.

Alex suddenly broke the gloomy silence. "I'm going to start a fire."

Archie and I snapped our heads towards him, who looked at us innocently.

"Ye dare not," I started. "Englishmen shall find us!"

"Aye, Marjorie, but we shall certainly perish in the cold. If the English find us, at least we have a chance. Alex and I are excellent swordsmen, and ye are a great bowman," Archie agreed, much to my dismay.

"Ye have a point. Get the fire going," I said, half smiling.

Alex nodded, then ran off in search of wood. I turned back to Archie, who was looking at me intently. "Ye know how much ye remind me of my own bairn, Marjorie?"

"Aye, Archie. Ye have told me many times." I giggled, hoping to relieve the tension caused by the conversation topic.

" I miss my beautiful wife and bairn every growing day. I shall never forget them," he told me with regret in his voice.

He cleared his throat, obviously giving the signal that he didn't want to talk about it anymore, and began on a completely new topic.

"Marjorie, do ye wish to aid yer father in his quest?" he said, shocking me.

"Aye, of course. I wish to have an army of my own and fight with my father," I said, smiling.

"Fair enough. Alex and I have been talking, and we have our plan set out for ye," Archie said, continuing: "We shall ride to Methven, where that first battle was fought. After a few days' rest, we shall set off for the Scottish coast, where clansmen may pledge allegiance to ye if they wish. Clan after clan we shall raise, but they shall not speak a word to anyone outside our army. After that, I do not know where we shall go, but all I do know is that we must go into hiding.

"When yer father calls on us for his aid, we shall go to him, although he will not know that ye lead the army. It is the safest plan. Do ye agree, Marjorie?"

I sighed as I thought about the possibilities this opportunity could hold for me. My dream of becoming a warrior had come true, and if I accepted, I could aid my father in regaining Scotland's freedom. We could finally be in harmony and peace. I would not be a woman growing old in the courtyard of Ayrshire until her dying day; I would be a princess who would forever be known through-out history for the deeds she had done for her country. I accepted my fate with glee.

"Aye, Archie. I shall accept this plan. 'Tis not for the faint-hearted, and I shall be risking my life for this chance to live freely. The risk does not matter to me, because I want the freedom with all my heart, and for Father to be happy as well. That is why I shall accept."

He smiled ecstatically. "That seals it then. We ride to Methven in the morn."

I nodded back before turning my head to the figure that now appeared out of the shadows. Bundles of wood were stacked up high in his arms, and I could tell the load was heavy because of the exhausted look that spread across his face. I stood up, about to offer a hand, before another tugged my nightdress.

"He can do it by himself, can't ye, Alex?" Archie chuckled heartily.

Alex said nothing but shot Archie a disapproving scowl. The wood was placed onto the leaves before us, and lit with the friction of another piece. Light brightened the dark woods, creeping into every nook and cranny that it hid.

Warmth escaped into the open air, and I no longer felt near death. I huddled up closely towards Archie, who was cradling Sorcha. Thoughts flew in and out of my head, causing me to shiver with both fear and excitement. As I fell asleep on my guardian's shoulder, one thought, no matter how hard I tried, would not leave me alone: *What is to become of me?*

The morrow came swiftly, and I greeted it with a smile. Alex and Archie were already mounting their horses and suggested I mounted mine, unless I wanted to walk.

What a sense of humour they have, I thought to myself, half-smiling. As I reached out to Ciaran, a quick glimpse of my hands proved how dirty I was. I needed to bathe desperately. Surely it was forbidden for a princess to become this dirty?

Smothering the final flame of the fire that saved us from our deaths, I then cast a number of rocks and leaves over the ash to cover up our tracks. This is what we had to do now because we were fugitives.

As we galloped away from the woods, it wasn't long before our nightmare turned into reality.

We had come across a small stream that drifted through the woodland. A hare bounded by, and sunlight crept through the canopy. It seemed too good to be true, and as we later found out, it was.

I dismounted first and ran to the stream, whooping with delight. Dunking my head under the water, I didn't waste any time in refreshing myself. I took big gulps of water, wanting to feel the cool delight trickle down my throat. Oh, this was ecstasy.

I bathed myself, rubbing all the greasy sweat and dirt off both my body and my nightshirt. I felt too vulnerable with men standing around me, so I dared not take the nightshirt off. It wasn't long before Alex and Archie joined me in the stream, also drinking and washing themselves. I refilled the water supply, and once I'd finished, I retrieved my bow and arrow and set off to hunt hare.

It didn't take long to get back into the hang of things. I had shot two arrows at a target in the tree above me, and both had landed exactly where I had aimed.

I was hungry and couldn't wait to get my hands on a tasty piece of meat. I needed protein, for I was weakening noticeably. Several hare bounded by, and I crouched into position. It seemed as if they were not wary of me, because they didn't even look surprised when a blessed arrow flew through the air, killing two with a single shot.

Before I could stand up and return the lithe corpses to my sack, the biggest male that I had ever set eye on bounded into my path. I smirked; this was going to be an easy kill. Taking a bow from my quiver, I crouched ever so low and drew the arrow back to my lip. It didn't need to go as far because of the short distance I was shooting.

Before I could let the arrow loose, a noise from the woods startled the massive hare. My eyes flew up towards the thick trees before me, searching in vain for the source. It certainly didn't come from Archie's direction. My thoughts were interrupted when a dozen or so men left the sanctuary of the woods to approach me.

"I wouldn't run, girlie," the tallest man said, slowly walking towards where I stood.

"We know who you really are," another added.

I stood there in shock, before deciding to continue the conversation in the French tongue.

"What do you mean, my lords?" I asked them nervously, my eyes flashing from one man to the other.

The leader smirked. "I mean," he said, before bowing mockingly towards me, "that you, my princess, have a price on your head for escaping Watton. And my boys and I are in some desperate need of money."

I spat towards the leader, showing my disrespect for his kind. *Fugitives. Bandits. Breakers-of-the law. Excommunicates.* There were so many names that I could think of, but one stood out.

Bastards.

"So now you come with me, girl, and do not put up a fuss, for I am making this easy for you. I can treat you worse, and I will if I have to," the leader demanded, breaking me away from my thoughts.

I began to walk towards them, an escape plan in mind, when I saw two figures approach the back of the group. Their swords were raised in the air, ready to strike. My two guardians silently moved closer, with looks of pure determination on their faces. They had heard the commotion and decided to check it out. Relief swept through me and almost settled with a grin on my face, but I dared not, for it would surely ruin the whole plan.

I did not cease walking towards them, but I had to figure out what I would do when the bandits began to realise that something was up. A yell silenced my thoughts, followed by a spatter of blood that ended one man's life. The leaders turned towards the newcomers, completely forgetting about me. Alex looked at me as if telling me that it was my chance to make a move. Quickly I fumbled an arrow onto the nocking point, and then all I needed to do was get the leader's attention.

"Over here!" I shouted, pleased to take all my anger out on this one man.

He turned around like a dog being summoned by his master. Actually, the similarities of that comparison were quite realistic. The leader did in fact resemble a dog. It was my time to shine.

The arrow shot through the air as the leader stood in shock at what came before him. He fell to the ground, dead. The next man turned to see the leader with an arrow piercing his eye. He choked up suddenly and began to bend over. Vomit escaped his mouth in a big, messy heap, but before he could stand again, I swiftly shot an arrow into the unlucky man's stomach, witnessing the unholy sight of his bowels escaping his body. Excrement stained the Englishman's breeches, and blood stained his torso. Alex quickly beheaded the man, relieving him of his pain, and kicked his disgusting body into the dirt.

I began to get back to work, unsheathing my sword, and helped Archie and Alex slice through the men until the entire band was dead.

Using one man's tunic, I wiped all of the blood that stained my sword and set off once again for the river, where my guardians were heading.

Looks like I need another bath, I thought wearily but triumphantly.
Marjorie Bruce

Chapter Seven

From the journal of His Majesty, Robert the Bruce of Scotland
  11th of March, 1307

Ever since that drunken night in Ireland, luck had been coming our way. My brothers Thomas and Alexander had successfully raided an English town, and I was awaiting news from them. Many Irishmen had come to pledge their allegiance within a fortnight, most claiming to come of their own accord. News had travelled fast to all corners of Ireland that I was here, and armies were turning up every so often.

With the blessing of King and Queen Ò'Neíll, Jamie and I, along with the nobles and their armies, left Ireland for the first time. The wives of the nobles stayed in the kingdom, although we granted Lord Hector O'Ryan the permission to stay with his wife in her time of need.

Five ships left the coast of Ireland two mornings later. Eighty men were on board each ship, which meant that I was taking twelve score of Irishmen to Scotland with me. This number didn't include my own army, whose numbers had lessened to one hundred sixty after the deaths of a few men.

On the day we set sail, the ocean did not want to cooperate with us. Wind sent the ocean up in arms, thrashing and flailing about under us. Many men, who had just completed an extremely long journey just to get here, disappeared under the deck.

I was on the largest ship, accompanied by my lieutenant, Jamie Douglas, and my third-in-command, James Stewart. The other noblemen that I had met in Tír Eoghaín also shared this ship with me, along with their lieutenants and commanders.

I had bought the ships off of an Irish merchant, who had also offered me the privilege of steering one of the ships. The merchant had sent word to his fellow captains, who had arrived a few days before we set off.

The days at sea were harsh, and the waves never seemed to fade away. Many of the noblemen, unused to travelling by sea, became seasick and were constantly retching off of the side of the ship.

Within a week, we were safely harboured off the coast of Ayrshire. I could clearly see Turnberry Castle in the distance. That was our destination.

Turnberry Castle is the ancestral home of Clan Bruce. It was our home, and it was where both Marjorie and I had grown up. Now because it was empty of Bruce blood, I had sent a few men ahead to warn the sentries of our forthcoming.

James and Jamie rode with me as we made the steep ascent towards my home. The nobles followed closely behind, taking in the new scenery.

"King Robert," one began. "You have a beautiful land here."

"Aye. 'Tis beautiful. The castle up ahead is my home, and ye are very welcome to stay there, if ye wish," I replied proudly, hiding a lopsided grin.

I began to gallop ahead of everyone else, before turning to face the hundreds of men I had bought together. I now stood in front of my home, and I couldn't help but feel proud that I owned this magnificent castle. It was time to introduce the men to Scotland.

"Today, we have reached the shores of Scotland," I shouted. "Many of ye have never set foot here before, and so I proudly introduce ye to our country. The castle behind me is my own, and my daughter and I have grown up here. Every single one of ye is welcome to Turnberry Castle, and as I speak, men are preparing ye quarters. Do as ye wish for this evening, but tomorrow I shall ask ye to assemble in the dining hall for a briefing. Off ye go, then."

Maids and servants rushed forward to help the men dismount, before taking their horses to the stables. As they walked through the castle gates, many gave me a nod or a small bow, to show gratitude.

I continued to ride into the village surrounding the castle, where I was met by the man who had minded the castle for so long.

His blond, curly hair had turned all shades of gray. He was getting old.

"Ah, Bishop. How nice to see ye again." I smiled, dismounting my mare.

"Robert." He nodded back. "I am glad to once again be in yer company."

He cleared his throat as I walked towards him, guiding the white horse along.

"Messengers have been through here many times, constantly updating me on what had happened. I am deeply sorry for yer loss, sire." He smiled sympathetically. "May they rest in peace, and may the Lord above welcome the Bruce brothers into His arms."

Bishop de Lamberton made the sign of the cross above his chest, before resting his gaze upon my mare.

"They, Bishop?" I asked, confused. "Don't ye just mean Neil?"

He gasped, shocked. He fussed around, placing one hand on his forehead and muttering to himself. I was starting to worry. He stopped in his tracks, before meekly looking up at me.

"I shall tell ye inside, sire. Ye may want to sit down."

I sat down on the dusty ground, many people stopping to look at me. Sweat began to pour down my face, partly because of the sun beating down on me, but also out of nervousness.

"Tell me now, Bishop," I demanded of him. "Ye shall not delay the news any longer."

"I hate to be the person who tells ye the dreadful ne—" he began, before I cut him off.

"Say it," I demanded once again.

"Yer kin, Thomas and Alexander, have been captured and executed by the English, sire."

It felt like the ground below my feet were crumbling and I was falling into a black abyss that held nothing. Tears formed in my eyes, and I couldn't hold them back. It had only been a week ago that I had heard from them, and they had been perfectly fine. I couldn't stay here, in sight of the public; I had to mourn in private.

Three of my kin had now been torn so brutally from their life, and for no reason other than me. If I hadn't been chosen as king, they would still be here, and so would all my loved ones.

I could barely stand up, and I could tell that I was paling. The bishop, obviously aware of the job he next needed to do, helped me to the door of the castle.

Once I was inside, I began to weep uncontrollably. The bishop had acquired the attention of everyone in the courtyard, and started to speak.

"The king has gone into mourning; he is not to be disturbed," he announced loudly, which caused whispers and mutters about the crowd to start up. I would now be the gossip of the village. That was just how life worked.

I stumbled up the stairs, trembling in my boots. I not only wept for Alex and Tom, but also for the hurt that the English had caused us. Tears glistened in my beard and lined my eyelids. I immediately ran to my quarters, which I hadn't seen in a year. I shoved my head into the white cotton pillow and cried my heart out.

I refused to wake up. I did not wish to accept reality at all.

In my perfect world, the kingdoms of England and Scotland ruled side by side, hand in hand, perfect harmony. Men and women could raise their children without being killed by the opposing country. Men would not have to leave their families for war, and brothers and friends would not die in vain.

But on Earth, that world could not exist. Countries were constantly at war, with men being killed, families torn apart, and homes burnt.

All I wanted was peace. All Scotland wanted was freedom. Why did Edward have to take it away from us? What was so bad about us, about Scotland, that Edward had to kill innocents and tear them from their lives ?

Greed.

Edward has everything he could bargain for. A beautiful country, beautiful women, buckets and buckets of money, and the crown of England. But he wants more.

Everything he already has is not enough for him. We could no longer wake up knowing that we were going to lead a perfectly normal life. No, he ruined our safety with a click of his fingers, and we couldn't do anything about it.

I wanted to stay in that warm bed all day, dreaming about a world that could have been, but duty called for me down in the dining hall.

I rubbed my eyes as I walked down the brightly lit corridor. slowly realizing it was already late in the morning.

Shite! I am late!

I turned the corner to see the men I had summoned observing the sight of me. My hair was rugged, my tunics were unorganised, and I could not think straight. How was I even supposed to address these men in my condition?

I wandered up to the dais and cleared my throat.

"Ahem," I began. "I have summoned ye here this morning for a briefing on our quest. Firstly, I shall need to update ye on the current circumstances."

No one said a word but kept listening to what I had to say. I looked around the room and then turned to Jamie, on my left. He offered me a sympathetic smile, as I prepared to relay the devastating news.

"My daughter, my queen, and my sisters have been taken prisoner. My English nemesis, Aymer de Valence, has them tortured endlessly to reveal important information about our position. So far, nothing has been said."

This news raised a gasp from the onlooking crowd, even more so from the men who had met Marjorie.

"Also, my lieutenant's brother, Archibald Douglas, is unaccounted for. His body has not been found at the site of the battle."

At the recounting of this, I saw Jamie cross his chest and say a prayer.

"Finally, this is the most recent of the news," I said, but as I continued, I could not help but release tears.

"My beloved brothers, Neil, Alexander, and Thomas, have all been captured by the English and, as of yesterday morn, executed." I choked up, unable to speak anymore.

Jamie approached the centre of the dais and ordered me to sit down. I had told him of all my plans, because he was the man I had trusted the most. We had known each other since we were wee bairns; our parents were always together.

I rested my head in my hands as he began to talk.

This is Edward's way of defeating me. By killing off all of my family.

Robert Bruce, King of Scotland

From the journal of Marjorie Bruce
2nd of April, 1307

We arrived in Methven only two days ago. Even though it had been left alone by the English, not a living soul called the ghost town home.

The rotting corpses that I had seen a year ago had decomposed down to bones. Birds and dogs no longer gnawed on them. In fact, according to the number of dog corpses that were strewn around, I believe that they all died out long ago.

The empty houses that lined the streets were beginning to rot, too, and old blood stained the ground.

The familiar inn was untouched, everything perfectly in shape. It scared me out of my wits, because this town was just too... silent.

The four of us made our way through the main street and into the inn. By tying the horses in the stables, we'd be sure that they wouldn't be seen by anyone. As a treat for Ciaran's excellent behaviour on the ride, I gave him a carrot that I had spared. He looked delighted as he fed out of my palm.

The beds were still intact as we raced our way up the stairs, and we longed for any sign of luxury. Sorcha, finally free from Archie's protective grasp, began to run around in the room we had just found, squealing with glee.

Not only were we protected here, we were also within reach of comfort, and we could hide comfortably. Alex's eyes were beginning to sag, the signs of fatigue were already there.

What we all needed was some quality resting time, and as the moon shone through our hotel window that very night, our wish was granted.

The next morn, I got up at the crack of dawn to investigate the ghost town properly. Archie and Alex were still asleep, and I daren't wake them. The wooden bed creaked as I rose from it, revealing a shadow of dirt that had left my feet overnight. A thin nightdress was all that I had to wear, alongside a thick fur blanket to keep me from freezing during the night.

The window was open, leaving the opportunity for the morning sun to enter the room. A light breeze brushed my skin and sent shivers down my spine. My matted blonde hair shook with the breeze, sending ripples of lengthy waves down my back.

I shuddered at the bites of the wind, leaving me helplessly cold. I crossed my arms, hoping to relieve the feeling somehow.

Turning from the window, the five-year-old orphan was sitting on my bed, gazing intently at the town below. Fiery red locks fell to the sides of her face, making way for two big, green inquisitive eyes. I knew that she would be a beauty, and when she came of age, all the men would be after her, despite her illegitimacy.

She jumped off of the bed, eager to follow me in my journey. She wandered up to my side, where her small head only reached my waist. I took her hand in mine and led her out of the room quietly. Sorcha was a quiet girl. She never talked in the presence of men, even Archie and Alex. Perhaps she feared them, for the male gender were the ones who murdered her family.

Down the stairs I led her, into the open streets of Methven. Barefoot, we trudged through the muck that littered the street. Coils of rope were on the ground, supposedly the remains of old washing lines.

Silently, we approached the end of the main street, which led into woodlands skirting the borders of the town. Without hesitation, the two of us stepped off of the dirt and into soft grass. Our bare feet soaked in the morning dew as we breathed the sweet air. The scent was unfamiliar, although it somehow reminded me of the honeysuckle-smelling soaps that I had bathed with as a wee child.

As we walked onwards, the grass became soggier, and the ground turned into a small marsh. Snapped twigs told us that many men, maybe a hundred or so, had been here, possibly within the past year.

Water inundated our small feet, which gave us a sign that a stream was flowing nearby. Our best chance of finding it was to follow the water, which is exactly what we did.

Grabbing tree branches to steady our footing, we easily arrived at the stream, which was only a league away from the main track. All we had to do was follow it back, and we could return to Methven safely.

Large trees sheltered the fresh river from any sunlight. Reeds grew in between the two banks, and pebbles lined the riverbed. I saw Sorcha gawking in awe at the sheer beauty of the place surrounding us. Algae grew on the rocks that jutted out, and fast, rushing water took part in pouring over top of the edges.

What a beautiful place to be, I thought contentedly.

Tranquillity seemed to be the subject of this woodland. Every now and then a butterfly would flit past, basking in its beauty. A chorus of birdsong left me in wonder as they left the trees to sing the song of the morning. I truly could not have been any happier.

Sorcha removed her tattered nightgown, the one that she had been wearing for weeks, and placed it on the riverbank. Without removing my undergarments, I did the same. Wading into the cold river, I assisted Sorcha in washing herself, before moving on to my own body.

Using algae, I scrubbed and scrubbed at my face and body until it was removed of all dirt. It took a long time to wash the remains of the algae off, because I had no tools except my bare hands.

I retrieved a piece of charcoal from the pocket in my nightgown. Elizabeth had always taught me to clean my teeth with charcoal, even though I despised it greatly. I winced at the aftertaste and immediately dunked my head underwater to get rid of it.

To my right, Sorcha had taken the task of washing the muck out of our nightgowns. She had grown since the day at Kildrummy and although she is small, that heart of hers sure isn't.

Underwater, I ran my hands through my scalp, parting all the knots and rinsing all of the grease out of it. Debris now swirled in the water below as I tried to splash it away from me. My hair now felt lighter and looked much, much brighter.

I closed my eyes for a moment, submerged in the tranquillity around me. It didn't take long for thoughts to fly into my head, clouding the memory of the river. Before I could fall asleep, a nudge at my side ceased my mind from wandering any further.

"Marjorie," Sorcha whispered, her deep green eyes staring into my soul.

"Aye?" I replied.

"'Tis a dead lad over there."

"Are ye sure?" I said, getting redressed into my nightgown once again.

Without saying a word, she led me over to where the bones of a man lay. He had been cut in half.

This is where the battle took place last year! I realized. I remembered watching that man fly over the English ranks to his death, just before I was found by the archer.

Leaning forward, I brushed the hilt of his sword, pulling it partly out of the scabbard. It was a short sword, meant for fighting in the shield wall. I had no use for it, and Archie and Alex had their own swords, but Sorcha still needed one.

Behind me, she knelt down as I turned and placed the sword on her shoulder. She giggled helplessly.

"I now knight thee, Sir Sorcha of Bruce," I said as I touched her other shoulder and her head with the tip of the sword.

Once we'd finished bathing, Sorcha and I began the short walk home, back to where Archie and Alex were still sleeping.

Marjorie Bruce

From the journal of His Majesty, Robert the Bruce of Scotland
6th of April, 1307

After Jamie had taken over my speech that morning in Ayrshire, we had all been dismissed to our private chambers to pack as much supplies as possible. The following days were spent in mourning for the lost, although I decided not to pay much attention to the ladies who threw themselves at my feet in despair. It was not their place to mourn; it was mine.

On Friday I took three hundred men, including the noblemen, with me to a small glen in the hills of Galloway. Our task was to win back the Scottish town of Cairsphairn, which had been taken by the English two months before.

The woodland was so vast that it took at least a week to cross, and although we were planning to stay in a village near Carsphairn, nature took its toll on us halfway through, and we were made to abandon the mission.

We had not nearly enough supplies to ride back home, and so we had to wait in Glen Trool until reinforcements arrived. This minor setback would cost us months, even more time away from my loved ones. I had to defeat the English one way or another.

Night fell on the hill where we slept, and stars emerged among the darkness, a sight that made us gaze in awe. Fires were still burning, and the smell of cooked meat wafted through the camp, tempting us all. Beautiful, burning embers flew up into the night sky as the blaze crackled all throughout the night sky. We fell asleep under them.

Rumour had spread throughout my men that the English were making their way toward Glen Trool. They wanted a battle, which we would have the disadvantage of, because we were weak and lesser in numbers.

I surveyed the land before me, breathing in the frosty morning air. From where I stood, a vast loch spread to my left, and to my right, woodland. Upon the hill on which I stood, a narrow pass led all the way around the loch. Consequently, this meant that if the English were to come, they would have to file through this narrow pass. If that deduction proved to be correct, it meant that I had the greater advantage, and with both hands I would grasp it!

Ten days after the English had started to march they had arrived in Glen Trool. I had ordered a band of scouts outside of our borders to update on any suspicious activity, and they had returned to report that the English were approaching hastily. They did not know of our whereabouts or the plan I had to ambush them.

Climbing the steep hill once again to witness the arrival of the English, I saw Aymer de Valence riding ahead of the cavalrymen with an air of arrogance, certain that he would succeed and trample our small garrison.

My men had been taken into the woods by James Stewart, my most experienced commander. There they would wait for my call before surprising them with an attack. I was to lead the first charge with only thirty or so men, and once they had retreated far enough, Jamie Douglas would take his part.

From the top of the hill, the Scottish archers lay in wait for my signal. I was with them, hiding under the scrub, where all my men kept a wary eye on me. One, two, three hundred cavalrymen rounded the corner of the loch, riding towards my men, who hid above them. All fifteen hundred Englishmen had kept coming until they stopped metres away from our hiding place, awaiting their next orders.

I could tell that not a single man suspected an ambush that day.

I looked over my shoulder to my archers, who had their bows at the ready. Heart thumping in my chest, I raised my hand up to signal the archers. They each placed an arrow on the nocking point, and as my hand came down, they loosed. Arrows flew down the hillside and into unsuspecting Englishmen.

One jumped from his horse with a scream before running straight into the loch. Others did the same, obviously thinking that water would relieve the pain. It didn't. The men who got hit with the first flight died; we made sure of that.

Archers were still loosing, many now standing up, watching their victims suffer. I stood over the men, ready to make my call for reinforcements.

"NOW!" I shouted, and just as I did, Scotsmen emerged from the safety of the woods, wielding swords and shields. The archers made way for the battle-hardened men as they leaped over the top of the hill, skidding down the side to make contact with the enemy.

Clashes of sword upon sword and axes upon shields rang all throughout the small valley. Helmeted men thrust forward, hoping to spear someone on their way through. We were fighting at the top of the slope, which gave us the advantage. Men were cut down from the ranks and murdered, blood smearing the pathway. The whole mass of humanity screamed with bloodlust.

As Jamie's men galloped around the corner, the English knew that we had won. Men ran into the loch, hoping for escape, but were instead cut down. The only man who escaped that day, just as the doomed Englishmen were being rounded up, was the man who had commanded it all: Aymer de Valence.

Jamie's cavalrymen rode around the group of three hundred survivors, jeering, mocking, and spitting. As my men slowly wandered down the hillside, we joined in the humiliation too. They were doomed, and they knew what was to happen to them. Dishonouring them as bastards, I slit every single man's throat that day for defying the king of Scotland. I made sure that the last thing they saw was me, and not their bloody English king.

Fortunately, none of my men had died that day in Glen Trool. At worst, they were injured and had to walk with a splint. They could not fight in the head of the army for at least two months. We rode back to Ayrshire immediately, malnourished and on the verge of death.

Robert Bruce, King of Scotland

Chapter Eight

From the journal of Marjorie Bruce

25th of April, 1307

Life was easier in Methven. We were still on the run, but no one would suspect that this was our hiding place. It all seemed like a big game of hide-and-seek, something that Father and I used to play when I was a wee girl.

Sorcha and I would go to the river every single night at dusk to rid ourselves of the dirt that inhabited our bodies. In a routine fashion, Archie and Alex would leave immediately as we got back, travelling to the river to wash themselves as well.

Most nights they would hunt boar, using the darkness as protection from our enemies, and that would become our breakfast, lunch, and dinner throughout the next day. Sorcha and I were usually asleep by the time the men got back from their little hunting trip.

Each morning, we would rummage through a different house every day, hunting for clothes, weapons, food, anything. Archibald and Alexander had found new clothes almost immediately, whereas it hadn't been so easy for Sorcha and me.

One morning, Alexander and Sorcha took a walk through the woodlands, rummaging for edible berries, while Archibald and I searched through another house.

This one was different than the rest. It hadn't burnt down like all of the others, and was standing magnificently in its place, almost inviting us in. Tattered curtains stood in the doorway, a result of a break-in and a long, slashing sword. This had happened most recently, possibly a few weeks beforehand.

The glass in the windows no longer remained, causing a blast of wind to seep into the house. It was cold in here, and I do not believe it was the wind that caused the hairs on my neck to rise.

We wandered cautiously into the next room, looking for positive trails that screamed *human*. The curtains were billowing, the breeze dominating this room as well. A table sat in the centre, basking in the sunlight. Piles and piles of herbs lay upon it, drying out with every day that passed.

I grasped the herbs in my hands, feeling the weight of them crumble into nothingness as I held out my hand. Flakes drifted down into the floorboards, revealing something that I hadn't noticed before.

Blood.

Specks trailed around the room before turning into blood-red footprints. I followed them all the way to the outside of the house, which left me with a ghastly sight.

I strode over to the wounded girl, who happened to be barely breathing. As I approached, I noticed her condition, which made me feel terribly sick.

Blood pooled around her feet as she lay in a patch of dirt. Her long brown hair was laced with beads of sweat as her heart beat faster, frightened of me. Long, sleek arms were draped around her stomach, where she clutched an arrowhead.

I whimpered, almost as if I could feel her pain myself.

"Archie! Archie! Come quick, I need yer help!" I shouted desperately, as I heard his footsteps echoing on the wooden floor.

"Marjorie, be qui- oh." His face dropped as he saw the girl in her state, looking miserably up at me.

As I lifted her head, waves of curls drooped down to her side. She was extremely beautiful, and I guessed she was about eighteen.

Archie leant in to help her up, and their eyes met. I knew at once that I would not be his favourite girl anymore, because it seemed as if he had another lass on his mind. That thought did not bother me.

The girl, doubled over in pain, winced and bit her lip, as though she refused to say anything. Archie hoisted her into his arms, looking down on her affectionately, as we ran into the house, frantically searching for a dressing that would be of use.

In the nearest bedroom I had found a washcloth, along with many dresses which lay in a heap on the floor. Later, I would ask permission from this girl to borrow some dresses, but I wasn't focused on that.

On the opposite side of the room, an empty bed sat waiting for its owner to return. The kilt that lay on top of it looked vaguely familiar. I thought that I'd seen it somewhere before; I just couldn't remember where.

I entered the front room, where Archibald had laid the girl on the wooden table. She was now pleading for relief.

"Marjorie," Archibald started, causing me to lose my thoughts, "ready Ciaran for me, please."

Without a further thought, I knew what Archie was intending to do.

"Aye."

I ran towards the inn, where my black stallion waited patiently. Ciaran was mine, but I'd have to give him up this once if the girl was going to survive. After saddling him, I stumbled inside to search for food. A dozen apples and two legs of boar would satisfy them for the journey. They needn't go far, only to the town that sat on the border.

I brought Ciaran to Archibald, who looked content with the position he was in. *Always the knight to rescue a damsel in distress*, I reflected fondly.

As I bid them farewell, the girl turned her head and smiled sadly, before nodding at Archie. Without looking back, they both rode off towards England.

Now how am I supposed to explain this to Alexander? I thought as they disappeared from my view.

Marjorie Bruce

From the journal of Archibald Douglas
29th of April, 1307

I hadn't loved for so many years, not since my Anna had died while in labour with our child.

Now I seemed to be happy once again, riding along the countryside with this beauty. She had barely spoken a word since we left.

She almost drove me wild with desire every time I caught hold of her sweet, sweet scent. I could not lay a hand on her, for the fear of rupturing the wound even more was ever so large.

We had ridden for three days straight, only ever stopping to relieve ourselves or eat. Luckily, we hadn't been stopped by Englishmen, unlike the journey I had made with Princess Marjorie.

On the fourth night, we had arrived at a small English town, known for its healers. Unlike the town I had travelled to in August late last year, this one had no gates and no guardsmen. It seemed as if they thought that they were immune to the bandits that roamed the paths. Their foolish decision left a major opportunity for the girl and I to enter the town.

Leaning in close, I whispered to her gently, "Ye know that whatever I say in here will just be an act. I am here to keep ye safe, not hurt ye."

At the sound of my voice, she hesitated, then nodded. She knew that I would need to be ruthless to her and she would have to play along.

Dismounting Ciaran, I tethered him up under a tavern, where I helped her dismount safely without hurting the wound anymore.

As I took her arm in mine, I pushed her long, brown locks away from her eyes. They shone in the moonlight, and I just wanted to whisk her away right then and there, but she would have to heal first.

"Ye know, I never got yer name." I smiled at her, tempting her to tell me. She smiled back.

"'Tis Aileen, Archie," she said sweetly, testing out my name.

"What a beautiful name for such a bonny lass," I said, and it was then that I vowed that she would be mine.

Placing a kiss upon her soft, pink lips, I cupped her chin in my hand as I did the same to her forehead. Cradling the young woman, I carried her to the doorway of the small house. At the entrance to the house, I carefully put Aileen down on her feet. Grabbing the hem of her sleeve, I pulled her roughly into the brightly lit room.

Glass jars sat on shelves, accompanied by herbs and plants of all sorts. In the centre of the room, linen had been thrown all over the floor. A fire was burning fiercely by the window. It was a small cottage, one that a lady would dream about settling down in and starting a family. But we weren't here for that.

I cleared my throat, a simple gesture that guests had arrived.

"What can we do for you?" a hoarse voice called from another room.

It only took a minute before a plump lady ran out from the room, a wide smile upon her face.

"She has been wounded ," I said, once again speaking in the French tongue that was so well known to the English subjects.

The lady's face dropped when she saw the state that Aileen was in.

"Won't be long, I assure you. Just have to finish dressing another man. I'll be with you in a second," she said grimly, before rushing out of the room.

I helped Aileen lie down in a comfortable position. I had a slight feeling that the lady didn't feel hatred for Scotswomen and, in fact, liked them.

This could make the situation a whole lot easier to deal with, I reflected as the lady, Ethel, burst back into the room.

Brushing Aileen's soft hair out of her face and making sure her husband was well out of earshot, Ethel placed a hand on her stomach and began to talk to her.

"Lady Aileen, this will not be an easy task to heal you. If we continue, you may become barren," she said softly.

I gulped. No lady would ever want to hear that she could possibly prove to be barren. It was their worst nightmare. Kissing her hand, I realized something.

"Ethel, how did ye know Aileen's name?" I asked, completely confused.

The two women simply smiled at each other before Ethel explained.

"Aileen's mother and I have history. She was my best friend and my maid of honour. I remember when Emma would bring young Emmeline and Aileen around all the time, but that stopped when Emmeline was bought by King Robert as a slave."

I caught my breath. *For the love of God, have mercy on these two poor innocent souls, for I do not have the courage to bring them such devastating news.*

Breaking me out of my thoughts, Ethel continued, smiling.

"Just as I know who you are, young Archibald. Guardian of Scotland, you are on the run as fugitives from England, just after you broke Princess Marjorie out of Watton. So, do please tell me how Emmeline is faring. I've heard that she is with child. Good on her, I say!"

My heart leapt out of my skin at the same time as my eyes bulged from their sockets. *She knows who I am! God save me if she tells anyone where we are; it will be the death of us all.*

"That young girl with ye, Archibald? That was Princess Marjorie?" Aileen exclaimed, completely speechless.

"Aye, it was," I started, before bracing myself to share Emmeline's fate. "Emmeline. Uh…four children, she had given birth to. Sorcha, Donald, Connor and Evie, if I remember correctly. She married a Norwegian man by the name of Alvar, a fine lad he was. Herself and Marjorie were the best of friends, and Marjorie would look after her children some times." I smiled, remembering the carefree girl Emmeline was.

I could see that Aileen had tensed up, and sweat was pouring down her forehead. Her hands were clenched, and I could tell that she was in immense pain, physically and emotionally.

"Ye speak of her in past tense. Did something happen to sweet Emmeline?" she interrupted.

"Aye. Both Emmeline and Alvar were killed in Kildrummy by the English. We tried everything, but it was just too late. Three of their children were killed also, but when I found them all, I buried them as a family, so they could be together forever. I am so, so sorry, Aileen."

Aileen choked up at this, and tears began to fall down her soft face. I hung my head in respect for Emmeline's family as they took their time to mourn.

"Thank you, Archie, for everything. I shall not tell anyone of your whereabouts or this little rendezvous. I'm sure that I can treat Lady Aileen, but you better both act English around my husband, or he'll have you straight to the king," Ethel told me softly, before continuing.

"Archibald, take a rest in the guest bed. It is just around the corner there. Lady Aileen shall be ready to travel by morning, I promise you."

"Aye," I replied, before Aileen grabbed my hand. I turned back to see her doe brown eyes staring back at me.

"What happened to the fourth child, Archie?" she asked, pleading for answers.

"Sorcha is fine and well. She is in Methven with Marjorie and my cousin Alex at the moment. She has the most beautiful red hair," I said.

"Sorcha..." she whispered as I walked quietly into the next room.

Archibald Douglas, Guardian of Scotland

From the journal of His Majesty, Robert the Bruce
8th of May, 1307

After the battle in Glen Trool, we had marched back to Ayrshire where fresh recruits replenished our stocks. Once we were settled down for at least a month of rest, we learned that the English had begun to march towards Kilmarnock, a large town in East Ayrshire.

The English were numerous even after their loss at Glen Trool: three thousand men compared with our six hundred. We had to keep our winning streak up because we couldn't afford another loss. It would ruin the Scottish army for good.

Rain bucketed down on the battlements of Turnberry Castle as we readied to leave. All of my men made up the cavalry line while the Irishmen were behind as foot soldiers. It would take at least three days to march to the location, and that was excluding any trouble the English might give us.

We were miserable and wet, the archers unhappy that the rain would affect their majestic longbows. Deciding to ride, I turned to face the men that stood behind me.

"Today we ride to Kilmarnock. Three days it will take to get there, and I ask for none of ye to delay.We shall ride and defeat the English in this battle, which is hopefully the last. Once this is finished, I shall relieve ye of yer oaths to me, and ye can go home to Ireland. Once we arrive at the battleground, I ask for ye to complete the tasks of which I shall instruct ye." Turning back to face the empty road that awaited us, I realized that this was going to be a long ride.

Kicking my feet into Isabella, she reared as I grabbed her reins and began to canter. Soon all the cavalrymen behind me did the same as we set off into the bleak light of day.

Racing down the path, I quickly realized that I was no longer alone. My hair stood on end as fear prickled inside of me. Expecting an ambush, I unsheathed my longsword and swung it around to tear into flesh.

Clash!

My sword met another's as I turned to see who the intruder was.

Fear darkened his brown eyes as they met mine, then glanced to the sword that I held at his throat. I took the sword back and sheathed it before glaring angrily at the man who rode before me.

"Shite, Jamie! I almost ripped out yer throat. Ye could've been more careful!"

"Aye, Rob, sorry about that. Ye got to be more trustful of people," Jamie remarked, grinning sheepishly, which only made me even angrier.

"TRUSTFUL?" I shouted, taking Jamie aback.

"How can I be trustful when my whole family has been taken away from me? When my own sisters were used to capture my daughter and wife? When three of my own brothers, as well as a brother-in-law, were captured and executed? My maid and her children were murdered, because I *was* TRUSTFUL! Yer brother is probably dead and mutilated right now, because of me! So if anything, I have to be less trustful!"

At the mention of his brother, I realized that I had made a huge mistake. I did not mean to hurt him at all, let alone yell at him. My temper had just exploded.

I could see the hurt in his eyes as he turned away, trying to avoid my gaze. Tears formed and began to fall down his face and into oblivion.

"Och…Jamie, I am terribly sor—" I started, but never finished as he kicked his stallion into a canter and rode off until I couldn't see him anymore.

I slumped in defeat. I was tired, moody, depressed, and now I had probably lost the closest friend I had. I needed him back, desperately.

The army was behind, catching up rapidly. I could not let them see Jamie or myself in this state so I cantered up the hill to where he was sitting.

In between the trees, Jamie had tethered his stallion to a thin strip of wood and was sitting underneath the canopy.

Dismounting Isabella, I wandered over to Jamie, who did not look up at me.

"Jamie, if ye wish, I can relieve ye of yer oath to me," I started gently, quietly hoping that he wouldn't.

As he glanced up in disbelief, I sat down with him to resume the conversation.

"Shite, Rob, I would never do such a thing!" Jamie began. "I just needed some time to myself, ye know, to get my head around some things."

"Aye, Jamie. I am terribly sorry about what I said to ye before. I didn't mean for ye at all to get upset, and I regret deeply about mentioning Archie," I said, taking scattered breaths.

"Nae, 'tis not yer fault at all. 'Tis Edward's," Jamie said, saying the English king's name with utter hatred. "And ye know that I shall always be yer friend, as we have been since birth. I'll always be there for ye, no matter what. I shall always look after young Marjorie, and when this whole war is finished, we can live in peace."

"Aye, and the same to ye. Now shall we go and kill some English?" I grinned, happy that our argument was resolved.

I helped him up and gave him a long hug, the one brothers would give upon being reunited after an extended period of time. We may have looked nothing like brothers, but we acted like it.

Helping Jamie up onto his horse, I slapped the stallion's rump cheekily, and I mounted my own.

Happy beyond words, I grinned sheepishly and rode off with Jamie Douglas by my side.

Robert the Bruce, King of Scotland

11th of May, 1307

We arrived at our destination only two days ago. Jamie and I were on speaking terms, although I did feel a pang of guilt every time I spoke to him.

It was not the time for mending broken hearts, though; it was the time for tactics and bloodshed. And so on the tenth of May, I led my army into battle.

Arriving first, we again had the advantage of higher ground and the element of surprise. I had ordered all the garrisons to build trenches just above the summit of the hill, which would soften the effect of the first charge.

Men were polishing their armour and weapons, readying themselves for either life or death. Brandishing their longswords, the Irish spearmen took their place behind the archers and cavalry. One hundred black stallions lined the hilltop, and in between each one, an extremely skilled archer made his stand.

My foot soldiers stood on each flank, wielding the bright red and yellow shield that bore the lion the kingdom of Scotland knew so well. These men would attack the flanks, hopefully leading the English into an early withdrawal before they made a fatal impact on my six hundred or so men.

Walking amongst the ranks, I had to make the final inspection before the battle started. From the east flank, I could hear the sound of drums and fanfare, which celebrated the arrival of the opposition. My men hardened their faces and unsheathed their swords before realizing that they were waiting for us to attack.

I turned back to my third-in-command, James Stewart, who looked content at the size of the English army.

"We will win," he said confidently.

"Aye, but how?" I replied, scanning the grounds.

"They took the route through the marshland instead of approaching us from the other side of the hill. The marshland has affected their numbers immensely, and Valence will nae be able to deploy his forces any further. They will be stuck, and we can attack the west flank with archers while we can surprise the foot soldiers on the east side," he concluded, pointing to where we were to attack.

"And the English cavalry?" I asked.

"The archers and cavalry are our best chance at succeeding in that area. The trenches that we have built will surprise them and hopefully lead them to their deaths. That is all I have in mind, sire."

"Thank ye, James. I dinnae know what we'd do without ye," I said with sincerity in my voice. I nodded at him before informing my other ranks of what we were to do.

It was time.

An hour later, I rode downhill with Jamie to meet the English commanders and discuss the terms of battle.

I rode Isabella, Marjorie's mare, and Jamie rode his stallion. Halfway downhill, three men approached in chain mail and the typical English helmet. I did not recognise any of the men until the visors were lifted and we could see their faces.

One man, tall and weedy, I recognised as the earl of Lancaster, and the other two had to have been Aymer de Valence and Humphrey de Bohun.

In Valence's eyes I saw bloodlust and confidence, as if he had convinced himself that he was going to succeed. I let out a snort, and his beady blue eyes narrowed and glared back at me.

"What amuses you, coward?" he said mockingly, spitting onto the ground beside me.

I ignored him before looking at the other two men, smirking. This action would stir them up, and they would be too angered to realize that we would surprise them.

"Thomas, Humphrey, how are ye, lads?" I said, smiling.

Humphrey returned a growl.

"You shall refer to us as 'sir,' you little piece of dog sh—" he said venomously before Jamie intervened.

"And ye shall refer to the king as 'sire,' *Sir* Humphrey, son of a bastard," Jamie retorted smugly, matching Humphrey's tone.

I grinned at Jamie; he sure knew his way with words. Jamie returned my smile, knowing that he had won by the way Humphrey shrunk back.

Aymer, however, rode forward, close enough to thrust forward if he needed and kill me off. He looked into my eyes, not happy with Jamie and me. Ignoring the whinges of his companions, Valence began to talk directly to me.

"Coward, I just want to let you know that my men and I *will* crush you, one way or another. I shall get your bastard friend here to die for all that he has said towards *Sir* Humphrey, and I will make sure that by the end of this day, *your* head will be resting on the end of my sword and you shall go to *Hell*." He sneered, half expecting me to take this insult to heart.

Instead, I chuckled heartily as if this was all a big joke. No man could insult me, no matter how wise or powerful. It just didn't hurt me at all. When I failed to react further to his tough words, Aymer slunk back to his men with a sour expression on his face.

Although I had acted like I'd taken absolutely none of that seriously, I had taken one insult to heart: the slur on Jamie. I would do everything to make sure that my friend was safe and away from that turd Humphrey.

But if everything went my way, Humphrey, Thomas, and Valence would be dead by the end of the day and their corpses fed to the wild boars from the woods.

And so on that day, when the trumpets called for victory, I unsheathed my sword, and we rode courageously into battle.

Robert Bruce, King of Scotland

Chapter Nine

From the journal of Marjorie Bruce

13th of May, 1307

I had no idea that the girl Archibald had rescued would end up to be my maid's sister.

The thought blew me away, and although I felt a longing to actually talk to her about Emmeline and about her past, it was still too early to mention her deceased sister.

I still sit and cry whenever I remember the poor girl and her final moments on that fateful day in Kildrummy. To be gone at such a young age...I ponder upon the thought of my own age at my demise. Hopefully I will not be so young.

No word has been heard of Father, not even when Archibald took Lady Aileen to the small English town. No one knew where he was or what Archibald was doing, and I bet my life that absolutely no one cared.

The reunion between Sorcha and Aileen was heartwarming, like mother and daughter reuniting after a long period of time. Sorcha had absolutely no idea that the woman standing before her was her kin until a few words were exchanged between them.

Words that changed everything in a heartbeat.

"I am yer aunt, Lady Sorcha MacNeil. Yer grandmamma was a very noble woman, as was yer mother, and as ye shall be, Lady MacNeil."

Sorcha looked up but gave no response or even a glance that held emotion. Instead, her sparkling green eyes locked onto Aileen's as she bent down into a curtsey. Finally, she spoke.

"Me mother was kind. I miss her."

"Aye, little one. Yet she is always in our hearts, here," Lady Aileen said as she caressed Sorcha's hand and placed it on her chest.

Grinning from ear to ear, Sorcha curtseyed once and ran off back to Alex and Archie, who were too busy swooning at the bonny lass before them to realise that the little bundle of fire had ran back into their arms.

I heard a growl from Archie and a playful chuckle from Alex, which indicated that they were both fighting over who would take Aileen. After we had eaten, a decision had been made about where we were to start acquiring troops. We were to ride to Mull, where we had allies at Duart Castle with the MacLeans. Long have they been friends of the Bruces, and long have they served Scotland in many wars. They are our strongest allies and have men aplenty.

The next day I took Sorcha hunting out near the river. Half the day was spent killing as many deer as possible, and the other half gutting them. A dozen would last us halfway to Mull, and we would be able to restock whenever it was deemed necessary.

Arriving back in the town with bloody arms and plenty of deer, both Sorcha and I were astonished to see Archie and Alex sitting on the gravel sewing gowns. Aileen was checking on them every few minutes to make sure that they were stitching correctly.

Never had I known a male that had embroidered or sewn before. It was suggested to be strange for male soldiers to do anything that had a feminine air to it. They say it is just not right.

Yet four simple but serviceable gowns they had made by the end of the day. One a pale white nightgown, a pale blue nightgown, a lilac day gown, and an iridescent green one. Being generous, I let Sorcha have the two smallest gowns, leaving me with the lilac day gown and the pale blue nightgown, small enough to fit my slight figure.

We were to ride out that night and so Archie and Alex began to pack up while Aileen, Sorcha, and I headed down to the river once again.

It was dark as we approached the soft waters of the river. A fresh breeze wafted through the trees as the glow from the full moon delved in and out of the still water. Insects flitted about, frogs croaked, but this moonlit bath by the river made everything bad in my life go away for this moment of peace.

We washed our hair and scrubbed our bodies, ridding ourselves of all the grime and dirt that covered us. Aileen stripped us of our tattered, old nightgowns and washed them in the river, before tearing them to pieces.

Not looking up from where they lay lifeless, she began to talk.

"My darling girls, what now lies before ye is yer past life, the life in which ye were trapped, unable to escape from King Edward. This is where ye leave yer lives, here, torn up by this riverbank, never to return again.

"Yer paths from here will lead onwards, towards a brighter future where yer future son, Princess Marjorie, will become king of Scotland and rule in peace, where ye shall sit beside him as the king's mother, knowing that ye raised him to be the boy ye always wanted."

Turning to Sorcha, she said: "And ye, my beautiful lady, shall marry a handsome knight, and ye shall live with many bairns in peace and be closely tied into the royal family. Ye were never born to be a slave, darling; ye were meant to be noble, ye were meant for greatness, ye were destined to rid this beautiful country from the tyrannous Edward Longshanks.

"Ye two will rid this kingdom of both him and his son, and don't let anything get in yer way."

All of a sudden I felt a fire burning inside of me, something that I had never felt before. Deeply moved by Aileen's speech, I knew that this was what I was meant for. To lead a great war band against the English. And do it I will.

It is custom for every married girl to wear her hair up under a cloth, and unwed girls to wear theirs down. That night I could not have cared less. After we donned our nightgowns, Aileen made sure to braid both mine and Sorcha's hair; we would ride faster if it weren't falling in our eyes every time we turned.

I took my time in braiding Aileen's hair, wanting to perfect it so the men would spend most of the night swooning over her features. Finishing off the braided bun, I pulled a few strands out from the side and paced backwards to signal that I had finished.

We strode out to where Archie and Alex were waiting, three beautiful horses at the ready. I made sure that I was to ride Ciaran by myself because I loved the individuality. Alex helped Sorcha up onto Briana while Aileen struggled to mount the chestnut horse that held Archie.

Her wound made it harder for her to mount horses and ride, so Archie placed Aileen in front of him and held the reins from behind. An obviously jealous Alex kept sending his cousin murderous gazes as Aileen got comfortable in his grasp. Responding to his glances, Archie kept winking cheekily back over his shoulder.

I could tell that Aileen knew that she was being fought over, for every time that Archie grasped her waist tighter, her cheeks flushed bright red. I had to get these two men out of their fantasy world and back into reality.

"Archibald, Alexander! Let's ride!" I shouted as I kicked Ciaran into a gallop. Wind pushed past me, giving me a sense of freedom that I hadn't felt for a while. It felt so nice after the river bath; my skin was cool to the touch and my nightgown flowed as I rode through the gates of Methven and out into the open.

Marjorie Bruce

15th of April, 1307

We rode all through the night and all through the morning, not stopping until Aileen could ride no more. I could tell that all the physical activity was making her suffer, and she had a pale, deathly look about her.

Only a day and a half into the ride, Aileen had come down with a fever. This was most likely the effects of the surgery, and she was worrying excessively about proving to be barren. We had to get to MacLean land quickly before she expired.

Her eyes were no longer a deep brown but verging on grey; her lithe figure grew smaller until she looked like the gaunt figure of Death himself. Yet Archibald still cared for her, and so he would until her final breath.

We had to continue onwards. Even Aileen knew that it was the only way of saving her. So we rode hard and fast towards Duart Castle, where Lady Fiona MacLean would be able to fix her, until we came across a small river that blocked our path.

Crossing would be dangerous, considering the fact that we had absolutely no clue how deep the bottom would be and that we risked losing the horses in the process. But we had no other choice. The men dismounted and steadied the horses, while we women also pulled our weapons out in case of danger.

Rolling up their muddy breeches, Archie and Alex worked together to wade the animals across, with us women still on horseback. Water splashed continuously onto their backs, leaving a pattern of tiny little dark spots on the dirty white tunics.

I could feel the lumps rising on their skin as the water became chest high. Any deeper and the current would be impossible to cross. I clutched my arms to my chest for warmth as the murky liquid welled at my feet, gently skimming the top. We were almost halfway through when I remembered to worry about Aileen.

Looking over my shoulder, I could see her quietly studying the movement of the horses ever so carefully. Managing a quick glance, she smiled tiredly at me, and I knew that she was having trouble staying awake. She knew what was coming if we didn't get help soon.

We eventually crossed the river and ended up drenched from head to toe, standing at the foot of MacLean land. A league of wild, green grass stood swaying in the early morning's breeze, paving the way that we had so long wished to see.

Both Archibald and Alexander led the horses up the winding road, and I sighed at the scenery that unravelled in front of me. I hadn't seen the ocean for at least one year, yet here I was standing right in front of the tranquil, rolling waves and steep cliffs that bordered the pebbled beach below.

I was suddenly disturbed from the peace as townsfolk came rushing out to see what all the fuss was about. I dared not reveal my identity, for the English would find me and capture me easily, so I covered my face with my hood. Any passerby would assume that I was nothing more than a slave travelling with her masters.

A voice barked from behind me, and I turned to see the tall, muscular MacLean chief staring up at me from the ground. His eyes seemed to know everything and yet tell nothing at all. I could see why they called him "John the Black" because everything about him screamed *mystery*.

I could tell that he knew who I was, even without anyone saying a word. It was obvious with the way he looked at me. Turning back to Archibald and Alexander, he gave a swift nod and gestured them forward.

"Welcome, good lads to the home of Clan MacLean. I am the chief, and anything ye would like during yer stay, come to me and we shall sort it out. I have ordered my men to prepare rooms inside the castle for both ye and yer slaves," he said, winking at me.

"Aye, thank ye so much, good chief. I trust ye know why we are here," Archie said warmly, grasping the chief's right hand and quickly pointing at Aileen.

John nodded and began walking with the men the rest of the way to the castle that awaited our arrival. I could still hear snippets of their conversation, although whatever they were saying, they were trying to hide it from the prying ears of townsfolk.

Uniformed men stood in rows, each one with a hand over their sword. Suspicious glances were given, and as soon as the chief came into view, their eyes snapped up and their backs straightened.

Two tall men stepped forward in synchronisation and pulled the brass handles on either side of the gate open, revealing the inside of the magnificent castle. I would have liked to stand there and gape in awe at the beauty, but we were not to linger.

Half a dozen ten-year-old boys ran out of the stables to our left and helped us dismount before leading our creatures back inside. I had no desire to leave Ciaran in the mucky hands of stableboys, but it had to be done.

The chief walked us in and shut the castle gate before calling out to his wife.

"Fiona! There is a poor woman who is in need of help, come quickly!"

Soon enough, a small, plump woman came running out from the hallway with three maids behind her. Her cheeks were flushed, and her face was almost pouring with sweat, as were the faces of the maids following her.

Archie slowly walked Aileen over to the chief's wife, telling her quietly that everything was to be alright and he would be with her soon enough. Smiling politely, Fiona took her gently in her arms and escorted her into another room, out of sight.

John gave Archie a reassuring slap on the back. "Yer lass will be alright, I'm sure of it. My Fiona has treated much worse, and they've all survived. Now, I'll give ye a chance to get cleaned up, and then ye shall join me in my chamber for drinks."

The men nodded eagerly, for they had not been able to have a pint of ale for weeks. I took Sorcha by the hand and led her up the stone steps, watching my feet for any protrusion that I might have fallen upon. Archie gave me a quick smile before opening the door for us and letting us in.

The room was complete luxury compared to the Methven inn.

Taking my hood off, I walked into the bathing chamber and was surprised to see a tub of lukewarm water sitting there. It wasn't long before Sorcha joined me, and we both began to wash ourselves vigorously.

It was still early morning when we had finished, and so I helped Sorcha change into her green daygown before putting my lilac one on. Combing her hair with a medium-sized brush that I had found, I had a sudden urge to braid her long red hair.

Humming the words to an old song my father had taught me, I took my time braiding her hair, taking in the warmth and beauty which surrounded me. I knew that we were safe.

> *I saw the wolf, the fox, the hare,*
> *I saw the wolf, the fox dance.*
> *All three were circling around the tree*
> *I saw the wolf, the fox, the hare,*
> *All three were circling around the tree,*
> *They were circling round the sprouting bush.*
>
> *Here we slave away all year round,*
> *So we can earn a few coins.*
> *And just in a month's time,*
> *I saw the wolf, the fox, the hare.*
> *There is nothing left,*
> *I saw the hare, the fox, the wolf.*

Twenty minutes had passed and I had just finished braiding our hair. We were now washed, dressed, comfortable, and presentable for our meeting with the laird. Reaching out for Sorcha, I led her back down the stairs and into the corridor.

We walked side by side for two minutes, looking for the cleverly hidden chamber that belonged to him. Finally we approached the thick mahogany door that was guarded by two well-presented guards. They looked us up and down once before barking, "Names!" and crossing their swords to bar our path.

I curtsied low and motioned for Sorcha to do the same. "We are invited guests of Chief John MacLean of Duart, my lords."

They nodded agreeably and released their swords from each other.

"Enter."

The door was pushed open, and the tallest of the two men entered the room, then stopped and bowed to the three men occupying the room.

"Good chief, yer guests await," he exclaimed.

John nodded quickly and then motioned for us to enter.

"Thank ye, Donovan. Ye may now leave," the chief said, pointing towards the door.

As soon as the door clicked shut, he stood up from his chair and knelt to the ground in front of me, acknowledging my presence.

"'Tis a pleasure to finally meet ye, Princess Marjorie." John said with a smile.

"Aye, same to ye, Chief MacLean," I replied.

With a flick of his wrist, the tall man insisted that both Sorcha and I take a seat next to Archie and Alex, who looked delighted with our arrival.

"Now, yer guardians Archibald and Alexander have told me everything that has happened and the plans for the future. Ye needn't worry about being safe, for I have doubled the guards since ye have arrived. Alexander has told me that ye wish for something of mine, Marjorie?"

Alex sent a cheeky grin my way, and I couldn't help but smile back.

"Aye, my lord. I wish for a score of yer best fighting men to fight with me against the English," I said hopefully. "We are on our way through Scotland to collect as many men as we possibly can, my lord."

He hesitated and then looked over at the men, who gave nods.

"Anything Her Royal Highness wants, she shall get. Donovan!" he shouted out into the hallway. It wasn't long before the guard entered once again into the room.

"Aye, my lord?" Donovan cried.

"Send for two score of my best men. They shall be ready to leave on the morrow with our guests. Tell them to bring a month's worth of supplies and to meet them at the gate on the stroke of midday."

"Aye, my lord," he said before exiting the room.

I looked at the chief in disbelief.

"*Two* score, my lord?" I questioned. "I believe I only asked for one."

"Aye, Princess. Although I do recall ye saying that ye need as much men as ye can get."

My mouth dropped open with delight at this offer, and at the reminder that I was somewhat royal. Joyously, I shook his hand until it was numb.

"Thank ye, good chief! How can we ever repay ye?" I asked cheerily.

He didn't waste any time in stating his reply. Placing a battle-hardened hand on my cheek, he looked directly into my eyes and whispered: "By winning this war, young one."

Marjorie Bruce

From the journal of His Majesty, King Robert the Bruce of Scotland
12th of May, 1307

It felt surreal. Surreal to be standing out here, waiting for the final call. Looking over at my men standing on the front line, I felt admiration for all they had done to serve me. I knew that some of those men had to die today, locked forever in the damned eternal shell of the unbreakable shield wall.

Jamie was mounted on his horse close by, in front of his assigned garrison. James Stewart had done the same, looking over once or twice to reassure me that the plan was going to be a success.

If this works, I thought, *I will give James whatever he wants in return.*

The Irishmen looked nervous, unsure how the size of our army compared to the English one. I was confident of victory.

Reflecting off of polished battle armour, the sun had risen high, showing it to be midday already. The English army was enormous, much, much bigger than ours. It looked menacing, almost evil, and I knew that if we succeeded today, then revenge was ours.

The slow and steady drumbeats sounded and rang across the valley, alerting any passersby of our intention. I could clearly hear the scrape of metal as the swords were slid out of their sheaths and into the hands of the waiting soldiers.

Silence swept across the valley with a movement so swift that it seemed that the very idea of sound was non-existent. The suspense was almost driving us to insanity.

"Die, you Scottish bastards!" Valence shouted from the front line of the English cavalry, instantaneously urging them to start riding with immense speed towards us.

Rearing Isabella up in the stirrups, I gave one last shout to my men and galloped forward to meet them with the rest of the cavalry.

Swords clashed against shields as the two opposing front lines met and a cry was given to James Stewart's archers to let loose amongst the English.

Valence had finally found me, and I made my way around to face him, clenching *Molreach* in my left hand.

Looking disgustedly at me, he thrust towards my torso and I immediately parried, glad to not hear the sound of metal piercing flesh.

I glanced over at the battle unfolding in the front line. My foot soldiers had finally found their match and were stabbing eagerly with force at the English while the archers were loosing frantically from the top of the hill.

Isabella suddenly kicked, and I looked back desperately at Valence to see that he had cruelly thrust his longsword into my mare's rump. Shouting with rage, I turned quickly and attempted to grab the bastard and kill him once and for all.

Parrying my blows, Valence cursed as I jumped on top of him and threw him off his horse. Landing on the ground next to him, his horse kicked and attempted to trample me. I quickly reacted and sliced *Molreach* into its throat, hearing the blood gurgle and its eyes turn white before collapsing on top of Isabella. Marjorie's Isabella.

With a new-found anger, I straddled the grimy, blond-haired Englishman as he struggled underneath me. Leaning in, close enough so that he could hear me, I whispered something that I had always wished to tell him.

"I told ye that if ye ever touched me lassie again, I would kill ye."

Slamming my palm into his neck, I thrust my sword deep into his chest. Blood spurted upwards, decorating my face and my sword in pure joy. This is what it was like to be a warrior. You fight for your kingdom, and you kill for your kingdom.

I had no other horse to substitute for Isabella, and so I had no choice but to fight on foot. Running back into the midst of the battle, I realized that the cavalry had all perished in the dangerous trenches that we had built. Broken horses lay in piles, and the once lush, green valley was now stained red with the blood of Scots and Englishmen.

I could distantly make out James Stewart as he secretly led his best archers along the west side. From where I was standing, it seemed that the English hadn't yet noticed that they were lining up for attack.

Once Stewart's men were ready, Jamie would bring his cavalry around from the east side to break the English and send them running back into their mothers' arms. Glints of sunlight reflected off of many of the Englishmen's polished armour, effectively blinding my footmen temporarily.

I thrust, sliced, and parried my way through the bloodshed, knocking them down so hard that they would never rise again. Many of the Irishmen fighting alongside me were putting up a good fight, although many of them had never had any training in the shield wall, and I could see that they were weary.

The Englishmen were starting to question the sudden disappearance of my two east and west flanks, and confusion marred the faces of all the armoured nobles atop their horses.

Suddenly, from the east, came Jamie and his men riding vigorously and angrily towards the English, hoping to break the soldiers up and slaughter a good many of them.

Surprised shouts rang out as de Bohun's men were effectively massacred in a number of minutes. This distraction proved to be exactly what we needed, for at the moment the foot soldiers were turned away, watching their comrades being killed, James Stewart's archers started firing from the west side.

Hundreds of bodkin arrows flew across the sky as my men retreated back up the hill. The back of the English army, the ones that had not faced us in battle, chose wisely and fled down the valley as the deathly arrows rained down upon them and pierced through armour and flesh.

"Retreat! Retreat!" the doomed earl of Lancaster called angrily to his men.

I laughed to myself as I cursed at the cowardly English.

"Ye better run! And tell yer bastard king that if he's nae careful, me men will be having his lassies in their beds!"

With a look of pure hatred, both Humphrey and Thomas muttered darkly to each other and rode off out of the valley.

I turned to face my men, not even trying to hide the pride that marked my face. Looking down at the dead warriors, I kneeled and clenched the grass, the whole time praying for their safe journey to the afterlife.

Soon all my surviving men had joined me and my eyes welled up as I realized that their brothers, best friends, fathers, and even sons had died here.

These men fought for me, and many of them died for me. And those who hadn't now had to live without them because of me.

Robert Bruce, King of Scotland

Chapter Ten

From the journal of Marjorie Bruce

15th of May, 1307

Chief John had sent emissaries earlier asking them for immediate assistance. If this operation was to be successful, then it would have to be extremely secretive, and absolutely no one could find out about it or know our true identities before reaching MacLean land.

We had been dismissed from the laird's room, Sorcha and I, after the men had had a little too much ale. While we down the corridors in fits of laughter with big grins on our faces, the light had all but disappeared over the rolling waves. A chill crept slowly but surely down my spine as I realized that we were not alone.

"What are ye lassies doing running around after dark!?" Donovan, the chief's servant, cried.

Startled by his sudden appearance, I grabbed Sorcha's small hand for reassurance and squeezed softly.

"Nothing, Donovan. My wee sister and I were just lost, that is all," I chuffed, unhappy with his inability to mind his own business.

With reluctance, he gave in. "Och, alright then. But don't let me catch ye out until the mornin'. There are lads around these parts who would nae hesitate to do horrible stuff to ye bonny lassies!"

And in the moment he strode away, I swear on Father's life that I saw a sly grin and a twinkle in his eyes. Scared out of my wits, I picked Sorcha up delicately and ran the rest of the way to our rooms.

Locking the door with a bairn in my arms proved to be challenging, and so I placed her down safely before finishing the task.

Little Sorcha looked absolutely exhausted. After today's events, even I was trying hard to stifle a yawn. I pulled back the linen and waited for the green-eyed girl to crawl in and lie down. This was a mother's job, but since hers had died I had adopted this role.

After changing from my gown to a pale white nightdress, I combed through my hair quickly and then extinguished the glowing embers of the fire. Silently tiptoeing around to the foot of the bed, I said a quick prayer for Father before climbing into the soft sheets.

The morning came with haste.

I woke to the sound of urgent knocking upon our wooden door. Wearily opening my eyes, I called for the visitor to enter the room. Sorcha's eyes were still fastened shut, and her little chest rose and fell with every breath she took.

A stout, pudgy-faced lady ran into the room, stopping to curtsey once in front of me.

"How is me lady faring this verra fine morn?" she asked politely, her country accent thick.

I bowed my head in acknowledgement.

"I am feeling fresh and renewed." I smiled back, to her delight.

"Verra well, me lady. I am required tae ask if ye would like tae join Chief MacLean and his other guests for a meal at midday," she gushed.

"We would love to," I reassured her.

Pushing her auburn hair aside, she simply nodded and picked up her skirts.

"I'll have someone send up some breakfast, a bathing tub, and some clean gowns for ye and yer sister. When that is done, I shall return tae escort ye tae the hall."

"Aye," I replied eagerly. "'Tis much appreciated."

Curtseying low once more, the lady walked briskly out into the waiting hallway.

The sunlight filtered through the dusty windows as I bathed in the warmth that engulfed my body. Sorcha was still fast asleep while I took the opportunity to witness the life of common people down in the courtyard.

As the minutes passed by, townfolk gradually exited their thatched huts arm in arm with their spouses. One or two children usually trailed behind them, eager to dirty their tunics by rolling around in the damp grass. Grubby-fingered girls clutched onto their mothers' arms while many of the boys ran ahead to greet friends.

Market stalls began to open, drawing potential customers from both in town and out of town to trickle in through the guarded gates. Prized vegetables, clothing, horse gear, weapons, and armour were bought with an exchange of a few silver coins. Bread-makers and blacksmiths worked away amidst the bustle of the crowd, strong arms kneading or hammering the objects in front of them.

Jesters entertained the women with amusing acts and stunts while the men entertained themselves with many pints of ale and drunken antics down in the tavern. Teenage girls looked on at the young men training in the fields, eyeing each one flirtatiously for the chance of a possible suitor. In turn the men, grinning, were enjoying the attention and the chance to show off their talents and muscles.

Just thinking of marriage concerned me. I had heard of many cases in which men were unfaithful to their wives. After the ceremony, men are supposed to be limited to only one woman to warm his bed, but many still take to prostitutes and brothels after becoming tired of their wives. If I was to marry, it would be to a faithful man who was honest in his ways.

I was suddenly chased out of my dreams by a shadow in the doorway.

"Milady?" the pudgy-faced lady questioned.

"Aye?" I replied, almost immediately.

"I have brought ye both a bowl of honey and oats," she offered, placing the wooden tray carefully on top of the dresser.

I nodded with appreciation, but before I could reply there was a sharp knock at the door, followed by a repeated *swishing* noise.

"Ah, that'll be the tub," the serving maid said, rushing to the door to assist the others. Two lean men entered with a wooden bathing tub and lowered it next to the hearth of the blazing fireplace. I could already feel the warmth of the boiling water.

As the two men took their leave, I quickly undressed and slid into the warmth. A sigh of happiness escaped my lips as the water quickly engulfed me. Sorcha opened an eyelid cautiously, and upon seeing that I was awake and in the bathing tub, she stretched.

A flurry of red hair bounced out of the delicate sheets eager to join me as the lady made her way around to my side of the tub with a hairbrush. Carefully running through my long hair with her fingers, she proceeded to untangle the unsightly knots and finally braid it. It took a good half hour before she wandered around to Sorcha's side. I saw a wince of pain sneak slyly out of her expression every so often.

We both finally stepped out of the lukewarm water and dried ourselves vigorously while the maid stepped out of the room to fetch something. Moments later she returned carrying two white, billowing and a plaid shawl for each of us.

We slid the gowns on comfortably in awe. It felt divine to be dressed in such beautiful clothing and attired with such traditional garments. Words could not express how proud I was to be wearing the tartan of my clan.

"Miladies, if ye would please follow me," the lady prompted us, beginning to make her way down the hall.

It was time. Time to meet the men who would fight alongside me and save Scotland from defeat. Men from every clan around the country would be there, although they were not briefed on their mission just yet. That was my job.

Wandering down the hall, my heart caught in my throat. At the other end of the passageway Archie had his arms around Aileen, a scandalous move if anyone saw them, and Alexander was looking disheartened already.

I ran to meet them with Sorcha trailing close behind. They would enter behind me and stand beside me to help if I needed it. A smile was instantaneously brought to Alex's face, and Aileen ran to hold Sorcha in her arms.

We waited there for minutes, listening to the muffled voices that arose from the large room in front of us. Some sounded agitated; others, eager to be here and get their orders. But none bar the chief and my company knew that I was going to be here. All expected me to be back in Watton, the hellhole.

Soon the crowd fell silent, and solid footsteps clear as day rang out as they approached the dais. A voice then broke the eerie silence.

"Dear friends! I am delighted that ye have come at my call. Please, fill yer starved bellies with ale and meat. But before ye do, I shall brief ye on yer mission, or rather, me guest will."

I could imagine the quizzical glances and arched eyebrows that were sent around the crowd.

The chief continued speaking. "It is me pleasure tae introduce ye tae the one who will lead ye against the English. Ye may know her as the princess of Scotland!"

Gasps went up around the crowd as I strode into the room, unsure whether to wave or simply acknowledge them. Most men stood in astonishment while the others shouted in anger at the chief.

"What is this!? A joke?" one man cried. "Our princess is locked up in Yorkshire, and ye mock her by bringing another lass in as a hoax?"

I looked at the chief desperately. This was going to be harder than I thought.

A voice cut in from behind me. "I can assure ye that this is King Robert's daughter, Tormod." It was Archie. "Me cousin and I were the ones who helped her escape from Watton. Just look at her. She has the late Queen Isabell's eyes and hair, does she not?"

The man called Tormod stood in silence, pondering this. "How do I know that ye are not lying, Douglas?" he growled defensively.

"Archibald is right, Tormod." Another man stood up. His face looked familiar, yet I could not put a name to it. "This is Princess Marjorie. I know because I was her father's right-hand man and her tutor in her wee years."

I gasped suddenly in amazement. "Chief Angus MacDonald!? Is that ye?"

"Aye, wee one. 'Tis years since I have laid eyes on yer bonny face," he said as he kneeled down before me.

"The princess has returned!" the chief cried in happiness as the men flocked to kneel at her side. Cheers went up around the room and left poor old Tormod MacLeod scowling in his seat.

After the uproar had died down, I was urged on to brief my men. All except Tormod were glad to join my company, and he was still forced to join and pledge his allegiance.

"Men of Scotland!" I began eagerly. "Ye have been called here because ye were deemed worthy enough to fight alongside me. I know that I am only a wee child, but I have not had the easiest childhood and have been trained how to fight. I never knew my mother, my best friend and my uncles were *murdered* for supporting my family, my father has been taken away from me, and if my plan is to be successful, no one must know that I have escaped captivity. *Especially* not my father.

"I was the one who stabbed Valence on that unfortunate day in Kildrummy and warned him that if he ever so much as touched me again, that I would vie for his blood. I am not as childish as ye may think." I took a moment to blink the oncoming tears away from my eyes. These memories welled deep inside me.

"Ye may have heard about my father's victories against the English at Glen Trool and Loudon Hill, but we are not to join them. That would only jeopardise our chances at defeating the English king once and for all. Ye see, I have learned his tactic. The Tyrant is taking me father's closest family and keeping them as hostages. He has already taken his wife and his sisters and killed his brothers.

"He took me as well. If my father finds out that I have escaped, he would find me and not let me out of his sight. In the event of an English ambush, I would be killed, and he would be instantaneously defeated because I am the last living and free person that he holds truly close to his heart. Scotland would fall. This is why anonymity is the best answer."

The room nodded in unison, still unsure of what to do but nevertheless understanding of the situation. Even Tormod gave an apologetic gesture.

"I hear that Edward Bruce is still alive, my princess," a surly man clad in armour stated from the back of the room.

"Aye, this is true," I replied knowingly. "And surely the English king will order his execution next. This is where the plan takes place." I stood back and took a quick glimpse at the parchment that had an outline of the mission.

"May I remind ye that ye are all under a vow of secrecy, and anything that ye have heard and will hear is not to be repeated out of these walls. Any traitors shall be tried and executed on the spot.

"We shall leave the chief's company on the morning of the eighteenth and ride hard for the Campbell land. This is where my uncle is residing for the moment. Under the guise of my father's men returning from battle, we shall not raise any attention and sneak Edward out. Sir Niall Campbell is here today and is willing to help the cause by housing us.

"After this is done, we shall brief Edward on the mission and send him to my father's army where he will be safe. He will not mention me, but he will tell my father to call on this war band when he needs us most. We will reside in Methven for the time being."

It was done. My speech had proved effective, and each man came to kiss my palm and pledge his allegiance to my cause. I had no more reason to speak, and so I stood back while the chief took over.

"May I thank ye for yer time, my men, and I should like tae remind ye that princess shall only be called by her guise, Lady Isabella. Oh and I am pleased to announce that Archibald Douglas and bonny Aileen MacNeil are tae be wed tomorrow eve! Ye are all welcome to join in on the merry occasion."

I squealed in surprise, although I had known that it wasn't long before the question was asked. Looking back over at the delighted couple, I watched Alex slink back into the hallway unnoticed by the cheering crowd.

Giving Aileen and Archibald a quick hug and my congratulations, I followed Alexander back to his room. Knocking twice on the closed door, it swung open to reveal a figure sitting by the fire with his head in his hands. I closed the door behind me and walked over to where he was sitting.

"What did I do to deserve such heartbreak, Marjorie?" he sobbed.

My heart ached for his hurt.

"Nothing, Alexander, nothing," I cooed softly, rubbing his back.

"Well, then, why did she choose him over me? Answer me that!"

"The heart wants what the heart wants," I explained. "They were in love from the moment they met, I'm afraid."

Alex laughed quietly. "Ye sure know a lot for a wee child."

"Aye, and don't ye feel down about Aileen. Fate will entwine ye soon enough with yer one true love. And in that moment, Sorcha tiptoed into the room and sat down on Alex's lap, her green eyes glimmering in the firelight.

Marjorie Bruce

17th of May, 1307

The morning of Aileen and Archie's wedding began with screams of pain from the street below. As is our custom, the groom was made to carry heavy rocks on his back up and down the dusty street until his bride ran out to meet him.

Unfortunately for Archie, Aileen is a heavy sleeper and did not wake until hours later when I was forced to get her up because I could not bear the noise anymore. By that point in time Archie was drowned in sweat and his muscles were aching tremendously; he had no more energy left for screaming.

Aileen, feeling guilty for leaving him out there so long, immediately ran and embraced him with a kiss on his dirty cheek. He cursed under his breath at the weight of the rocks, but returned her greeting by picking her up in her slender gown.

The rest of the morning was dedicated to readying Aileen for the event. For a girl of eighteen, she knew very little about traditional weddings.

Sorcha, Fiona, and I sat excitedly in Aileen's chamber while two maids ran to fetch the bathing tub. The bride-to-be was fidgeting nervously and playing with her long brown locks. Once the maids returned, we helped undress her and let her slide into the warm water.

"Fiona, ye are the only motherly figure I have at the moment, and I would love it if ye could give me away tonight," Aileen said unexpectedly.

Fiona, surprised at the request, gushed uncontrollably.

"Of course! I would be honoured tae give away such a bonny lass."

"Thank ye Fiona." She smiled. "And who could forget my beautiful niece and Princess Marjorie? Ye are the ones who saved me from a horrible, horrible death and brought me to my soon-to-be husband. I couldn't ever thank ye enough."

"Fate brought ye to us, Aileen," I answered simply, pride filling my heart at the beautiful girl unfolding in front of me.

"Alright now, enough chat. Aileen, I suppose ye already know what happens between a man and a woman on their wedding night?" Fiona asked in a motherly voice.

My cheeks flushed red, and Sorcha raised her eyebrows in a questioning glance.

"Nae, I cannot say I do, Fiona," Aileen answered sweetly but innocently.

Fiona also blushed. She said quietly, "Well then. I suppose that it is up tae me, but first, Marjorie and Sorcha need tae take their leave. I dinnae want to damage their sweet innocence with what goes on in the bedroom."

Aileen looked scared. She looked even more afraid when Fiona was done with her an hour later.

"Ye knew about these…proceedings?" Aileen asked, fear-stricken.

I shrugged the question off. "A lady I once knew was bought for bedding almost every night of the week. It was hard to avoid the subject. One night, because she was so upset about her body being sold, she opened up to me and told me *everything* that went on in the bed. I must add that I was quite disgusted and didnae plan on marriage."

"Prostitution is a horrible business." Aileen spat.

"Aye. 'Tis a disheartening subject, and that is why I planned her marriage with a good man. Her children were looked after by the other maids, so she didnae have them on her back all of the time."

"Aye. But let us not dwell on the subject, because today is a day for merriment and joy. Now, I suppose that Fiona is looking for ye. Yer dress is almost ready, I believe," I said, winking.

"I suppose ye are right. Farewell then, for I shall see ye tonight at my wedding! Enjoy yer day, Princess," Aileen replied, striding back to her chambers.

"I shall!" I called after her.

I found Archie in the gardens, deep in thoughts.

"'Tis a bonny morning, Marjorie." He smiled, greeting me.

I embraced him and grinned cheekily. "'Tis not as bonny as yer bride."

"Och! Stop rubbing in the fact that I cannae see her until tonight. How is she faring, anyway?" he asked.

I hesitated before answering. "She is fretting."

He frowned. "What is tae fret about?"

"She is worried about the wedding night. Ye know…the proceedings," I answered truthfully.

"Oh! I suppose that Fiona had a little chat with her, then. I wouldnae hurt her, not in my wildest dreams."

I nodded thoughtfully. "Ye better tell her that then. Make it known that she has the choice to go through with it if she wants. If she refuses, dinnae force her. It'll come soon enough."

"Thank ye, Marjorie." He chuckled. "So I expect that ye will join us at the wedding?"

Picking a handful of purple heather out of the soil, I handed it to Archie carefully.

"Wouldnae miss it for the world."

Evening rolled in over the hills and the wedding began. Faggots were lit, and blazing fires brought warmth to the waiting guests. Purple and white flowers layered the ground, and men and women had travelled from everywhere to witness the occasion.

Alex stood to the side of Archie, who was formally dressed in the Douglas kilt and tartan. Both men looked extremely nervous congregating with the priest. I stood to the side with Sorcha, trying not to draw attention to myself as the ceremony began.

The trumpets sounded, and a lively tune erupted from the local band. Everyone's head turned at the same moment to watch as Fiona walked Aileen down the aisle.

She was stunning. Aileen was adorned in a shimmering light blue gown crowned with flecks of gold. Her doe brown eyes emerged from under her cascading locks, her pink cheeks reddened in the firelight, and her smile could melt hearts. What a beauty she truly was.

As she stepped onto the dais, Archie turned to face her and simultaneously took a deep breath as he took her hand in his.

Pulling out a dirk from under his belt, he placed it in her palms gently.

"For our first-born lad." He nodded reassuringly.

"For our lad," she replied, smiling.

The priest then motioned for their hands as he wrapped a piece of Douglas tartan around securely. The vows were said, and so the priest joyously announced them man and wife and launched the celebration.

Six long, wooden tables were carried out laboriously into the courtyard, and tray after tray of hot food followed, the aroma wafting through and reaching my nose. Time to feast!

Snatching up a hot pheasant wing, I gave it time to cool as I made my way over to the crowded couple. I had the advantage because I was small and so I crawled through all the gaps, pheasant wing still in hand, until I came out the other side.

Archie turned his head and saw me, flashing an astonished grin.

"How'd ye get past everyone?" he questioned.

"I have me ways." I winked back.

I looked back at the crowd and suddenly realised what they were doing. A massive pile of presents stacked almost sky high was increasing every second. The people were giving their three gifts to the married couple.

I kept chewing on the tender wing as Alex found his spot right next to me with a huge pint of ale, frothing at the top. He ruffled my long, blonde hair eagerly as he held the flagon out towards me.

"Ye wanna try some?" he asked innocently.

I looked back to Archie and Aileen, who were too busy gazing at each other intently to realise what was happening right next to them.

"Aye!" I smiled and grasped the flagon with both hands. Taking a sip, I immediately choked up at the horrid taste. Spitting it back out onto the ground, I handed it back to a surprised Alex as I tried to rid the taste by downing some bread.

"I guess ye dinnae like it?" Alex grinned.

I grimaced "No. I should stick with water for now."

As Alexander and I dug into the delicious broth that had been prepared, I had the feeling that I was being watched. Looking directly across the table, I saw whose eyes were on me.

A boy, about my age, had met my gaze. He had bright red hair and eyes so blue that they almost challenged the ocean. After a minute of watching me, he turned to another red-haired man and whispered something inaudible. The man, who was probably his father, looked up and also glanced at me. He gave a grimace and whispered back to the boy, whose face dropped sullenly.

Through the night, I did not feel the boy's eyes break from me once. It was only until the music started playing that I could not find him amongst the crowd. I decided that he had probably retired for the night, but I was wrong.

Alex, Archie, and Aileen left the benches to join in on the dancing, leaving me alone with half a bowl of broth to finish. A moment later, the boy took his place next to me, cutting a piece of bread off of the loaf and chewing it contently.

"Lady Isabella," he announced.

I had almost forgotten that I was under that name as a guise, but I turned to face him and nodded. He leaned in closer, within arm's reach of me.

"Princess Marjorie," he whispered, his blue eyes gleaming, so nobody else could hear.

I gasped, sure that the red-haired man had informed him of my identity. My subconscious was telling me that I should be angry at this betrayal, but perhaps it was for the better that he knew.

"That is me name. And what may yers be?" I asked, smiling.

"'Tis Walter. I am first-born of James Stewart, right-hand man of yer father," he replied.

A wave of familiarity swept over me; Father had always talked of James. He was a good man and an excellent swordsman.

"James is in the company of me father at this very moment, so who have ye travelled with?" I asked, certain now that the red-haired man was not James.

"Me uncle," he said abruptly. It seemed he didn't want to take the conversation any further.

"Would ye like tae dance, Princess?" he asked, cheeks flushing red.

"No formalities, just Marjorie," I said, glad that I had found a friend.

"I shall take that as a yes," he said, winking at me as he grasped my hand and led me over to a patch of grass where many couples were dancing, already lost in the music.

Over his shoulder, I saw Aileen and Archie thank guests for coming as they ran upwards to Archie's chambers. I would not see them until morning.

Stepping in time with the beat, I let the princess inside of me go and became someone else. The fires blazed with warmth as he led me around in circles, dancing to the folk song. I could hear the drums beat around the courtyard and bagpipes play as all the guests joined in and lost themselves to the tune.

Hours passed by as we circled around the yard in unison, not worrying about anything else as the night sky engulfed us and embers from the fire flew into the air. Tapping my feet on the ground, I picked up my gown and twirled myself around.

He caught me by my waist just as the song ended, and I felt my heart speed up as he stole away into my eyes, not letting his gaze slip as he grinned cheekily. Picking up my hand, my heart fluttered as he placed a soft kiss into my palm before whispering in my ear gently.

"And me uncle said that I couldnae make ye mine," he scoffed, before smiling genuinely and running off into the night, leaving me to wonder about this strange boy.

Marjorie Bruce

18th of May, 1307

I spent the rest of the night in awe, thinking about the son of James Stewart. He wasn't traditionally handsome but there was something about him that attracted me to him slightly.

After Walter had left, Alexander had sought me out and danced with me for another hour before retiring. The fire's warmth was disappearing, and the sharp cold wind was settling in as Alex took me up to my chamber door.

It seemed that he had already taken Sorcha up a few hours ago, for she was nowhere to be seen. He turned and kneeled down to my level, all the while running his hands through his curled hair.

"Walter Stewart," I said, catching him by surprise. If anyone was to know about him, it would be Alexander.

He smirked. "Ah, I see that ye've made acquaintances. What do ye want tae know?"

"Everything," I said confidently.

"Well, he is yer age and heir tae the Stewart clan. When James passes, Walter will be laird. He is a real gentleman, that one. Also, he is here with his uncle to represent the Stewarts. Walter is travelling with us on our journey and learning the art of battle. It seems that ye both will be taught by me," he concluded, and my hopes began to soar.

I will see Walter again!

Feeling content, I bid farewell to Alex and slipped into bed cautiously, where I found Sorcha already snoring lightly.

It was still dark when Sorcha woke me, eager to get going. She handed me my lilac gown and helped me slip into it. Once she'd tied up the bodice, I helped her into hers.

We left the room for the last time, ready to embark on the next stage of our journey. I'd made sure that Archie had saddled Ciaran for me the night before, just before he left with Aileen.

Sorcha and I were to meet down in the dining hall, where we were to feast with the company before we left.

One hundred armour-clad men sat at the benches, stuffing their faces with juicy meat and crisp bread while others were stuffing their packs with food. My stomach rumbled as I found Alex and Archie amongst the bustling crowd.

Walking over to them, I noticed that Aileen wasn't there.

"Good morn!" I chirped, cutting up a piece of bread and swallowing it.

Alex nodded back and drank heartily from his flagon before embracing us. Archie just smiled like a content dog.

"Where is Aileen, Archie? Is she not well?" I asked, a hint of concern in my voice.

"Nae, I believe she is well. Just sleeps like a cat, she does," Archie replied with a sincere smile.

"Must've had a good night then," Alex chimed in, causing Archie to give him a death glare.

Archie changed the subject to our upcoming travels as we took full advantage of the feast in front of us.

After a while I felt a cold, large hand on my shoulder. It was Tormod MacLeod.

I turned to face him as he gave me a dark scowl. Behind him, a dark-haired, broad-shouldered boy of about fifteen approached to stand by his side.

"Ye listen tae me, Princess," he said disapprovingly. "I dinnae want ye getting close tae that Walter lad. Ye will marry me boy, and I will make sure of that."

"Ahem." Someone cut in from behind Tormod. It was Archie.

Tormod's scowl darkened even further.

"Tormod, yer contribution to the princess's marital affairs is not yer business, 'tis the king's. And if Walter wishes to court her, then so be it. Bugger off before ye offend anyone else!" Archie said, frightening everyone in the room in spite of his casual tone.

It got quieter after that, and quite frankly, I was scared. Scared that Tormod might force me into a marriage before I was of age, one that I did not even want to contribute to.

"Mighty men of Scotland!" the chief boomed, breaking the silence and the fear that had climaxed.

"Today ye leave for Campbell lands with the aid of the princess. Ye will travel in four garrisons, twenty-five men in each. In three days ye shall reach yer destination and take Edward Bruce outside of the citadel, where ye shall inform him of his quest. Pack enough provisions for a three-day ride and saddle yer horses, for ye leave now!" he cried with encouragement.

A rush of adrenaline surged through my veins as I raced out the door and into the stables to beat the stampede of soldiers that were making their way through the doors now. The sun was just rising and the sea breeze rolled in, making it a particularly cold morning. Ciaran was still standing there, his sleek coat looking shinier than usual against the dusty saddle that had been placed there overnight.

With my pack of provisions slung across my back, I led him out into the courtyard where a crowd was beginning to gather. A strawberry-blond stableboy stepped forward and handed me my quiver, bow, and longsword as I mounted Ciaran and waited to take my leave.

Horse after horse left the large, old, wooden stable, led by each man as he got his wits about him and mounted, ready to ride. A joyous cheer arose from the crowd when the chief emerged, acknowledging his loyal followers.

Kicking my heel into Ciaran, I urged him into the almost endless line of impatient men waiting to exit the gates. I was halfway in between the first and last man. Finally the bolted doors unlocked, and a unanimous rhythm began beating from underneath as we trotted out of the safety of the large gates and out into the open, awaiting our orders.

Two figures draped in black cloth sat side by side on a grazing stallion as I rode out to meet them, the wind gnarling my hair. It was Archibald and Aileen. Aileen looked like she could manage a couple more hours of sleep, but Archibald appeared as sharp and bright as the sun's piercing rays.

"Good morn, Marjorie!" Aileen chimed, shortly followed by a long yawn. "I assure that ye enjoyed the occasion last night?"

Alexander must've told her about Walter, I thought, well aware that my cheeks had flushed a brilliant red.

Archie hesitated, clearly unsure whether what came out of his mouth in the next minute would be good or bad in my eyes. He continued anyway, deciding to ask instead of leaving the question unanswered.

"Marjorie," he began, "it seems as if we are one too many horses short. I know this is hastened upon ye, but would it be too rude tae ask ye tae share Ciaran? Just for this ride?"

He stood there grimacing, waiting for the answer as if it was a life-or-death situation. Of course, if we left a man behind because of a horse shortage, it would do no good for the army. We needed every man we could get. I was also probably the only rider small enough to fit another behind me.

"I mean, we c–" Archie said, before I cut him off.

"Who is it that I have the pleasure of riding with?" I asked, hoping to God that it would not be the malicious Tormod or his evil-looking son.

A large grin grew across Archie's face, but I could see that he was still a bit nervous. So I gestured for him to spit the news out quickly.

"Marjorie, ye'll be riding with–"

"Me."

A light-hearted voice sounded from behind as I felt somebody jump onto Ciaran. The grin on Archibald's face widened as I turned to see those ocean-blue eyes from last night staring back at me.

Aileen cleared her throat. "Marjorie, meet the heir of the Stewart clan, Walter."

Riding with Walter had been pleasant to say the least. After we had left the company of the chief, the impatient riders had set off into the woods that roughly bordered the east side of MacLean land.

The original plan was for four discreet garrisons to be riding side by side, but it hadn't been long until that idea was thrown out of the window. Horses armed with men rode as far back as the eye could see, although there were little clumps here and there, chatting with their comrades as they rode into the morning sun.

As soon as we had started off, Archibald and Aileen had immediately kicked their heels into the sides of the young horse, sending it flying across the countryside and leaving me alone with Walter. I had no idea what to say. I had never thought that I would see him again so soon!

"We should ride," he said, breaking the silence.

"Aye, let's go," I replied before lurching forward in the saddle and kicking Ciaran into a fast gallop, hardly giving Walter any time to hold on.

Suddenly, I felt two gangly arms slither through the holes in my sides and rest contentedly on my waist. Turning my head back in the slightest, I saw the pure terror on his face as he held on for dear life, which only encouraged me to go faster.

I flashed him a malicious grin, and he scowled back, knowing that I had ridden fast on purpose. I slowed Ciaran down to a paced run, dropping back slightly, yet not losing sight of the rest completely.

We then passed out of the dim woods and into an open field where sunlight had just begun to pour deliciously in, drenching us in warmth. Walter let go of my waist, happy with the speed that we now rode at.

Three more days of this, three more mornings of watching the beautiful sun rise, riding through the golden fields. Yes, I could get accustomed to this.

"What's it like? Being a princess?" Walter suddenly asked, cutting through my visions.

"Oh, I'm not really the right person tae ask. I've only been one for a year at the most," I replied, curious as to why he would ask such a question.

"Yet ye are completely the right person tae ask. Ye weren't born one. Is it different from just being the first-born tae a clan chief?" he countered reasonably.

"Alright," I said, impressed. "I guess it is. Ye are expected tae be chaperoned almost everywhere, which I hate. I like freedom. I guess that is part of the reason why I'm also fighting for this country to regain what once was ours."

Walter's slow but steady voice made him seem like he was deep in thought. "Interesting," he said.

I raised my eyebrows. "What?" I asked in a questioning tone.

He chuckled simply. "Ye are exactly how me father described ye, except he forgot yer indescribable beauty."

This time, my cheeks felt like they were *blazing* red. I hurriedly faced forward, hoping he wouldn't notice how red my face had become. Urging Ciaran faster, I had to catch up to Aileen and Archibald by nightfall.

As the hours began to roll into late afternoon, I became exhausted. All my effort had gone into catching up to the pack, although I hadn't realized that I was physically draining myself. My mouth ached for water and my stomach for food as I slowed Ciaran into a halt.

Sliding off the horse wearily, I foraged around in my leather pack for the waterskin that had meticulously been filled with pure boiled water. Taking gulps of water and quenching my thirst, I offered some to Walter, who took it determinedly. Jumping back onto Ciaran, I secured the top and pulled the straps over my shoulders, a newfound energy burning inside of me.

We reached the camp just after nightfall, tired and weary. Although the fires were blazing and the men sat around gorging on meat, I felt the need to sleep. I took a seat next to Archie, Walter sitting by his uncle's side, and settled down under a piece of dark fabric. Resting my head down onto the dried-out, fallen leaves, I watched the glowing embers burst into the dark sky and listened to the soft chant of laughing men and old folksongs as I slowly drifted off into sleep.

Marjorie Bruce

Chapter Eleven

From the journal of Marjorie Bruce
21st of May, 1307

The sun still had not cast its shadow over the open glade where I lay. The crackling fire at the end of my vision was being tended to by three tall individuals, each holding bundles of firewood. Soft murmurs spread throughout the waking crowd, arms stretching up into the darkness in unison.

Alexander stirred, rolling gently over onto his side with Sorcha still firmly in his grasp. I studied him for a moment as he reached up to wipe his brow clean. Almost instantaneously, the nineteen-year-old's dark brown locks fell loosely down around his face, providing little protection from the blazing heat.

I stood up with ease, taking in my surroundings. Men had now risen and were beginning to ready themselves for the day's ride. Hauberks were donned and glinting swords scraped the edge of their scabbard as they slid in.

A sweet aroma began to fill the crisp air as day-old loaves of bread were rationed out to the men. A small pot of ale sat brewing adjacent to the fire.

"Yer Grace," a young voice announced groggily. "Would ye like tae break yer fast with me this morn?"

I turned to see a bowed figure standing behind me. It was Walter, wearing a lopsided grin as he rose from his gesture of goodwill. I had to admit, he looked rather becoming adorned with his hauberk, sword, and particularly dishevelled hair. Curtseying low, I took his arm and motioned forward.

"I would love tae," I replied, looking deeply into his smiling eyes.

We strode forward into the frenzy of men, each vying for the largest share of bread. Stepping forward over a warm puddle of ale, the man in charge of rationing handed Walter a small but pleasant-smelling loaf of bread and slyly snuck him a flagon of ale. If his uncle caught him smuggling the drink, only God knows what would happen to him.

He adjusted his arm so it fit perfectly in the nook of my elbow as we found a cosy log to sit on, not too far from the fire. Cracking the bread in two, Walter handed me one half as he began to chew his. The bread crumbled in my mouth, ceasing the loud rumble that usually echoed loud and clear throughout my stomach.

We ate silently and enthusiastically until Archibald greeted us, a sleepy Aileen clutching desperately onto the nape of his metal aventail to steady herself.

"Ye ready for the ride, Marjorie?" Aileen yawned heavily.

"Aye," I replied between mouthfuls of bread. "Are ye?"

Putting his arm protectively around his wife, Archibald shook his head quickly.

"Nay, I am afraid that *she* will not be joining us for the rest of the journey."

Walter and I both gave him a confused look as Aileen sighed and rolled her eyes.

"For all we know," Archibald explained, gently caressing her abdomen, "Aileen may be carrying a Douglas heir, and she needs not tae be riding from place to place. She will be safely escorted by three men of my choice tae Methven, and she will stay in their care until we arrive."

I nodded silently as the realization dawned on me. Archibald had lost both his first wife and child during childbirth, and he would do everything in his power to ensure that Aileen and the possible bairn were safe and out of harm. If she stayed with us, there was a definite chance that she could miscarry.

It seemed as if Aileen wished to add something to Archie's explanation, although whatever burned in her mind was quickly washed away by the arrival of Alexander and Sorcha walking towards us, her red hair more ablaze than ever.

"Morning Aileen, Archibald," Alexander acknowledged. "Marjorie and Walter." With that he hinted a sly wink in my direction.

I had a dark feeling in the pit of my stomach that everyone around me was *already* considering suitors for me. Father would have already arranged my marriage if it were not for the war that raged on.

Just to think of the subject and who my father may have picked out for me made me sick in the stomach. The worst he could do was betroth me to the son of wicked Tormod MacLeod, although there is little chance that I will marry before the war ends. If it ends.

Snapping back into reality, I realized that everyone's eyes were on me.

"I said shall we ride, Yer Grace?" Sorcha repeated, startling me.

Smiling, I nodded. "Aye, let's ride."

In the moments that followed, I heard Archibald shout something to the feasting men, who abruptly stood up and went about preparing their horses. Walter beckoned me forward, but Sorcha's pleading eyes begged me to stay back for just a moment, so I did. Walter went on ahead, disappointment clouding his eyes.

I kneeled down to her eye level and grasped her hands lightly. Leaning in towards my right ear, she whispered four words.

"Will ye marry him?"

I chuckled loudly, causing Sorcha to raise a questioning eyebrow.

"Sorcha, there are many, many years before I marry, but if ye wish it, I shall try my hardest for ye."

"Aye!" she exclaimed excitedly.

There was no chance that my father would betroth me to Walter when I could as easily be used as a pawn in a peace treaty.

After five minutes of wandering, I eventually found Walter sitting patiently atop Ciaran. As he held out his long arm, I grasped his wrist and used it to swing myself up onto the massive stallion behind him.

Walter handed me my longsword and my bow and quiver, which I gratefully slid into the scabbard hanging tightly around my waist. After readying myself for the sudden lurch into action, Walter dug his boot into Ciaran as we edged closer and closer towards the impending darkness of the night.

The cold, biting wind crept into my grass-stained gown as I gripped Walter tightly around his waist. Unable to bear the wind any more, I buried my face in the folds of his warm tunic.

As the sun rose, the weather fined up, and I was able to raise my head out from underneath the fabric. Walter looked straight ahead determinedly, keeping the same pace that we had acquired from the very beginning of the journey.

"Tormod MacLeod wishes to betroth me tae his heir," I stated innocently, waiting to hear his reaction.

Walter's posture stiffened, as if he had just tasted something bitter.

"Malcolm MacLeod will try tae seduce ye, make himself an heir and then kill ye so the MacLeod clan can take the throne for themselves. Dinnae fall for their good charms," he replied simply with distaste.

My eyes widened with surprise. Surely he could not do that.

"Well, that settles it then, I am never tae marry. I shall die an old virgin," I declared confidently, trying to humour him.

He looked amused. "Is this so? Then I shall have tae be ever the more charming than I already am if I am tae win yer hand."

On the third day I was exhausted. I felt as if it was beyond my ability to stay awake, and so I was carried onto Ciaran by Archibald.

He placed me in front of Walter, and I vaguely felt his arms loop through mine and onto the reins of Ciaran. As I drifted off into sleep, I could feel the morning breeze slip carelessly through the strands of my hair as the birds sang softly and sweetly through the vast expanse of treetops.

I felt as if I could decipher every melodic sound that the birds made, as if they were words themselves. One sang of tragedy, a daunting loss of life, while the others sang of birth, joyous times, and the blossoming of young love.

Soon I plunged deeper into the chasms of sleep, leaving this world far behind to dream of perfection, the things that would not come to life. For life isn't perfect, it never has been and never will be. The moment that I realized this was the moment that I realized that I would lose a lot more people who are close to me, like it or not.

I opened my eyes briefly, scanning the scene before me. We had stopped riding, the constant rocking motion no longer there to whisk me away to sleep. From what I could tell, it was now late in the evening. Riderless horses were grazing the fertile land for food.

The weight behind me now began to shuffle from left to right, unsure whether to help me off first or jump off himself. Deciding for him, I swung my leg around to the left side and launched myself off of Ciaran and onto the compact soil beneath. Walter looked surprised at my sudden movement, and I would have been too if a sleeping person just happened to jump expertly off of a horse and land on two feet.

He grinned and joined me on the ground, trying to find a place where we could easily conceal our weapons for they were surely not allowed in the Campbells' castle. The ground was cool under my bare feet as we discovered a cleverly hidden thicket amongst the borders of woodland.

After completing the task, we raced forward across the green fields towards a solitary wooden boat that awaited our service in the deep-blue waters of Loch Awe. In the middle of the loch stood Innis Chonnell, a large stone castle that had once belonged to Sir Niall's father, Colin Campbell, a personal enemy of my father.

Gripping the oars that floated lightly above the water, Walter and I stepped into the small boat and began to paddle our way towards the big island. The water parted gently at each delve of the oar, silence sweeping throughout the loch. After a while, soft voices could be heard from the gloomy castle towering above us, murmurs and mutters spreading about the advancing boat.

Breaching the shore, we jumped a short distance and landed in a small, swirling puddle of murky water. Walter and I approached the castle with haste, hoping that Archie and Alex had forewarned the inhabitants that we were still arriving.

The gate was open. I breathed a sigh of much-needed relief. Walter took my arm in his, and he began leading me under the raised metal lattice-like structure of the gate. We were inside.

The chill of the growing twilight air had been banished and was immediately replaced by warmer, stuffier air as the doors snapped shut. A tall, slim woman rushed hurriedly towards us, her dark, shoulder-length hair bobbing up and down amidst the bright lights of the hall.

"Lady Isabella, Lord Walter," she said, curtseying kindly. "Yer companions await ye in the dining room, they are all supping at the moment. Would ye care tae join them?"

I glanced at Walter, who nodded politely. "Lady Isabella and I would love tae. Would ye escort us?"

Turning on her heels quickly, she led us down the hallway and into a larger, brighter room filled with civil laughter and dazzling smiles. There the young maid curtseyed once more before running away, not giving us even a fleeting look.

Walter led me calmly inside, careful not to make too much of a ruckus. I searched the growing crowd of feasting families: men, women and children all shoving marinated meat into their mouths. Archie was seated at the far back of the room amongst his men, all quenching their thirst and satisfying their empty stomachs.

Slipping past Walter, I briskly strode towards Archie, keeping my head down just in case anyone should recognise me. Any of these noble ladies and lords could have been at court at the exact same time I was. Lifting up my gown, I seated myself opposite to him, smiling briefly at both him and the middle-aged man who also sat adjacent to me.

Archie's eyes met mine, and his face paled before straying to the stranger beside me. I raised my eyebrows suspiciously, wondering what on Earth he was doing.

"Marjorie." The stranger choked, turning slightly in his seat to face me.

Looking up slowly from my tray of food, I took my first proper glance at the deep-set blue eyes and unmistakeable red hair that belonged only to my father and his last surviving brother, Edward. And it definitely wasn't my father.

Marjorie Bruce

From the journal of Robert the Bruce, King of Scotland
8th of July, 1307

I stood tall in the courtyard, looming over the feeble page cowering in front of me. His face had been burned red over the many miles that he had scampered just to deliver the news that I had asked for. News of my imprisoned family.

"What say ye, boy?" I asked stiffly as he rose from his kneeling stature.

"Sire, I have the most rewarding news for ye, but first I shall tell ye of yer family," he replied, a grin stamped onto his face.

I grunted half-heartedly.

Brushing the grime off of his breeches, he looked up expectantly into my eyes. "Sire, Ladies Christina and Mary are still imprisoned in Yorkshire, Her Grace the Queen is also being held in England, but there are some rumours..."

I sent an amused glance back at Jamie, who had just happened to be with me when the page had called on me unexpectedly. He knew all of my secrets and darkest moments, and there was nothing that I was willing to hide from him.

Crouching down to level with the meagre boy, he looked concerned as I placed a strong hand on his frail shoulder. I felt as if I could snap his delicate body here on the spot.

"And what are these rumours, boy?" I said or killed.

"Sire, there are rumours spreading that the Princess Marjorie is no longer held in the convent and that she has escaped with the help of two of yer oath-men."

"Has this tale been confirmed by the English, boy?" I asked, beginning to fret for Marjorie's safety. If my little lass was all alone in the woods with two strangers, God knows what might happen to her. She is the last tie to my first wife Isabell, God rest her soul. My life wouldn't be worth living if my bairn was gone as well.

"No, sire. 'Tis just the talk of the Englishmen," he admitted, before hesitating. "There is something else, sire."

"No, my boy. I would like tae retire now," I cut in before he could say anything else.

His face dropped, but that didn't stop him from talking. As I turned away from the courtyard and made my way towards Jamie, my heart soaring at the confirmation that Marjorie wasn't by herself, he squealed: "Sire, I beg yer pardon, but it is of the utmost importance!"

Stopping in my tracks, I turned to see the little boy again kneeling at my feet. Jamie raised his hand to strike the boy for speaking out of turn, but I held him off, wondering what this little boy could possibly know.

"Rise, boy. If ye speak out of turn again, there is nothing stopping me from stripping ye of yer title. Now speak," I said disdainfully.

He rose from the ground, unable to hide his excitement at the news.

"Sire, I am pleased to announce that Edward Plantagenet, king of England, died on the shores of Carlisle yesterday morn. He was so weakened by dysentery that he perished in his servant's arms as he ate his morning meal. England is up in arms at his death, and they wish tae get his son Edward on the throne as soon as remotely possible."

My eyes widened in both surprise and joy at this news. I could not contain my happiness at this news. Jamie shouted in elation and clasped the boy to his chest.

The whole courtyard had turned to stare at our unusual behaviour. For a moment I had forgotten that I was king and was supposed to maintain a proper distance from my subjects. The crowd were staring expectantly, as if waiting for me to relay the news that had so suddenly brought me delight.

Jamie released the boy from his strong grasp and nodded at me to go ahead. Straightening my posture, I spoke to the men, women, and children who waited.

"Edward the Tyrant is dead!" I yelled before adding, "May Hell rot his soul!"

The crowd screamed in delight, and each spat on the ground as a sign of their hatred of the man who had separated families, killed their kin, and ruined their homes. Then they quickly scattered, running towards their homes to tell other members of their family.

Turning back towards Jamie, I noted that he had a sly grin on his stubbly face.

"What?" I asked him happily.

"Come on, let's go bring Edward and his father's ambitions down." He smirked, opening the door to the stairwell in front of me.

Moments later, Jamie was sprawled amidst the warm water in the bathing tub, which sat in the middle of the chamber adjoined to mine . As Jamie washed himself, I could hear every moan and sigh. It was not an appealing addition to our conversation, but nothing could dampen our spirits right then. I sat on the stone floor of my room, my head in my hands.

"Ye know what Ed will do next, don't ye," Jamie called out nonchalantly

"Aye," I sighed exhaustedly, running my hands through my long, red beard in deep thought. "He will ally himself with France by marrying King Philip's daughter, Isabella. That is evident."

Jamie made a sound, although I couldn't distinguish whether it was disgust or approval. "He'll also bring back that Frenchman, whatshisname, Piers. Piers Gaveston. He was exiled by Ed's father years back, but now that the king is dead and gone, there is nothing stopping him from bringing him back. Gaveston is one conspiratorial bastard."

"Mmhmm," I said, it all becoming clear in my mind. "Edward will give him a title and also marry him off tae some noblewoman tae keep him close and swarm himself with allies."

A splash sounded from the next room, signaling that Jamie was leaving the tub. It was my turn to bathe. He strode out of the room, half dressed in breeches, with his tunic hanging limply over a bare shoulder. He shook his head like a wet dog would do after a wet night, sending droplets of water all over the floor.

Rolling my eyes, I moved into the next room, disrobed and lowered myself into the steaming water. I didn't want to spend too long in there, as I was required in the dining hall to make a speech within the hour. Ducking my head under the water, I ran my hands through my hair to try to loosen the grease that had congealed on my scalp. The water burned my nostrils, causing me to emerge from under the water and start spluttering everywhere.

My lungs burned in pain, and tears began to well at the corners of my eyes. James entered the room hastily, snatching the towel off of my bed and helping me out of the bathing tub and into the room.

Sitting me down, he smacked my chest a few times to try to rid my body of the water that I had so foolishly swallowed.

"Better clean yerself up fast." He smirked. "For ye have a visitor."

I looked at him in disbelief. I had announced that I was going to retire and that no visitors should be admitted.

"I simply said just an hour before that visitors were tae wait until we had supped." I growled softly.

"Aye, Robert, but this is one visitor ye dinnae want tae miss," James said, his smile reaching the corners of his mouth.

I waved him off, and he ran to the door as I quickly changed into my breeches and tunic. No man should have to see his king in his own undergarments, but this was an exception. The poor man would just have to bear the sight.

James re-entered the room with a man of a broad physique, flame-red hair and cavernous eyes. A man so familiar in appearance that he could have been my twin.

"Robert, may I present Edward Bruce, yer younger brother." He beamed as my eyebrows arched in surprise.

Edward's eyes burned into my skull, and only then could I sense the familiarity that had been brotherly love so many years ago.

He ran forward as we collapsed into each other's arms, a wave of understanding engulfing us both as we began sobbing on the hard, stone floor. Memories came back to me of my childhood, when life was so easy.

"Here, Robert, pass the ball!" Edward yelled, running forward to try to elude the others. I threw the sheepskin ball violently as Edward jumped to catch it but was knocked back by Neil as he dashed in front of the ball and caught it.

"Neil!" Edward cried angrily, "ye cannae do that! It isn't fair!"

"I can do what I want, Ed. I'm older than ye, anyway," Neil countered, sticking his tongue out at his younger brother.

Edward scowled and scampered off towards where Mother sat in the garden, holding a suckling Elizabeth. Isabel, Mary and Christina sat with Mother as well, picking heather and making little floral bouquets.

"Och, Neil. Why do ye have tae be so hard on him?" I asked, despair racking my voice. All I wanted was peace and contentment between my kin, not hardship and suffering. Who knew what might befall my family in a lifetime?

"Robert, yer the one who is too soft on him. He needs to toughen up, otherwise he'll never be a good warrior," Neil said dismissively.

"Did ye hear that lad?" Neil called to Edward, who was now dancing with his sisters to an old folk song. "Ye'll never be a good warrior, ye'll never be a good man, and ye'll never get a wife! Ye will chicken out within the first few seconds of battle, and ye will be killed. There is no point in living if ye act like a woman yer whole life!"

I was appalled at the way Neil had acted. No one should have to listen to anything like that from his own brother.

I stalked up to where Neil was glowering and poked him hard in the chest.

"Shame on ye, Neil. No one should have tae be bullied into becoming who they are. Edward will come around eventually, and he'll be one fine warrior, ye'll see. He looked up tae ye Neil, ye were always the person that he wanted tae become, big, hardy, and strong. I'm nae sure if he wants that anymore, though, seeing as what ye just did. If ye ever speak tae him like that again, he won't be the only one who despises ye."

Spitting on the ground in front of him, I walked back down into the garden to comfort a sobbing Edward. Mother stood there with Elizabeth in her arms and a concerned look on her face. Mary, Christina, and Isabella all surrounded him, showering Edward with hugs and kisses.

Edward would always be the favourite.

"I hope ye put him in his place, Robert," Mother said knowingly, a small smile on her glowing face.

I nodded as I took little Elizabeth in my arms. "I did, Lady Mother." My youngest sister was so petite and blissful in her moment of sleep. I had never seen anything more peaceful.

"Would ye mind taking her to rest, Robert?" she asked.

"Of course, Lady Mother," I replied, turning away from the commotion in the garden and heading up towards the castle.

Inside, Thomas and Alexander sat on the wooden dais with Father, who was teaching them etiquette and how to behave in court.

"Ah, Robert!" Father exclaimed, before stepping off of the dais and walking towards me. "Just the person I needed."

"Whatever for, Father?" I asked, genuinely confused. Thomas and Alexander were already making their way towards me when they suddenly knelt.

"Pretend, Robert, for the moment, that ye are king of Scotland," he said, and I scoffed. Like that was ever going to happen.

"I am teaching Tom and Alex here how tae greet their king or queen at court. Nicely done, lads," he said, applauding them.

Waving them away, Father leaned close and whispered in my ear. "Now what just happened with Neil, Robert? He stalked in moments before and slammed his door. I am genuinely concerned about that lad."

"Aye, he was being too hard on Edward," I said simply, cradling Elizabeth who was beginning to wake. "He said that Ed would never be a warrior, never be a true man. I told him tae leave him alone and that Edward will come around sooner or later. He stormed off."

Father nodded and returned to Thomas and Alexander, who had begun wrestling over a piece of bread.

Striding up the stairs and into Elizabeth's room, I placed her down on her wooden cot and restoked the dying fire. I turned towards my sleeping sister and kissed her gently on her peanut-sized lips.

"Yer father thought that I'd make a good king, Lizzie. Alas, I am just an earl's lad, I may never even meet the king! What do ye think, Elizabeth?" I laughed before closing the door in front of me and settling down on the soft, comfortable bed adjacent to the cot.

Edward sat on the left of my bed, and James sat to my right. The feast had finished and the crowd had all but disappeared back home, so the three of us walked back to my chamber to speak of the past and what was to happen now that King Edward was dead.

"Robert," Edward began, "I've recently met with the leaders of a growing war band who are residing in Methven for the time being. They wanted ye tae know that they are at yer beck and call. They shall come and serve yer cause whenever ye should need them. Their numbers are growing by the day."

I nodded, wondering who it was that could muster such an army. "Do ye have any names, Edward?"

He shook his head hesitantly. "Nae, none were given. Although they did know who I was, if that is of any use."

I snorted. "Of course they know yer name, Ed! Yer the king's brother, every-one knows yer bloody name."

He flushed red, lowering his head into his hands.

"Is Marjorie with them?" I tried, looking for evidence that he was lying or hiding something.

He looked up quickly, frowning. "Of course not. She is still in Yorkshire with our sisters, is she not?"

"Aye," I said, confident now that he was not lying. He had not referenced the rumour of her escape.

Jamie interrupted, eyeing Edward slyly. "So what are we tae do now? Surely Edward will issue a peace treaty for a couple years, just tae sort his life out. Who do we fight now?"

"Right now Edward is not our enemy," I said slowly. "We shall take out the second biggest threat tae the Scottish throne."

"And who is that?" Edward said scornfully.

"All that are loyal tae the Balliol claim and who support the Comyn clan. Edward, ye need tae take charge of Galloway and make sure that there are no raids or sackings. Jamie—"

"—I'll rid Douglas Castle of the Englishmen. I have *some* men that are willing tae get the castle back," Jamie interrupted.

"Aye, I shall set ye up with one hundred or so men, is that sufficient?" I waited for his nod before continuing. "I will take the rest of my men tae capture Inverlochy, Urquhart, Inverness, and Nairn for the time being. I want *no* threat to the throne when I defeat the English. The Comyn clan fight a battle that I want no part in."

"They've been our enemies ever since that night in Dumfries," Edward added solemnly.

"Aye," I said simply, remembering that fateful night that I had sinned and become an excommunicate in the house of God.

Robert the Bruce, King of Scotland

Chapter Twelve

From the journal of Marjorie Bruce

  10th of September, 1307

"Left! Right! Left! Over! Right! To yer left! Under!" Archie screamed over our heavy grunts.

We were lined up in the open field, each parrying and defending ourselves with our trusty longswords. The grass was just beginning to stain the colour of copper, a sign that the harsh and hot summer days were ending and paving a path for the much more appreciated season of autumn.

As far as I could see, the men of Methven were already beginning to rise, sharpening and polishing their pickaxes and hoes with scavenged curtain cloth and loose rocks found in the bank of a small stream. Noblemen who once would never be seen working as serfs were now ploughing the fields, ragged scraps of clothing clinging to their skin like moths around firelight.

We were to inhabit this ghost town for months yet, which meant that everybody had to hold their own, no matter how highborn they were.

The sun was now sky high, a warning that the day was only to get warmer from here. I could feel, smell, and taste the sweat that laced our foreheads as we pushed on, eager to improve our chances of surviving a battle. Archie worked his way up the line, stopping once in a while to give us advice or correct us on our stance.

The man who stood before me—a man of about forty, more or less—looked disheartened to be fighting a partner of completely opposite size and shape. His salt-and-pepper beard coiled in copious amounts down to his shoulder, where a magnificent scar now healed to the right of his collarbone. I noticed after some time that he was limp in his other arm—the one that now dangled his shield down to his thigh.

Disregarding that deformity, he was extremely quick and skilled with his sword arm. I remember Archie telling me afterwards that he is known to the men of his clan as Dugald the Lithe—a fitting name for a man of his standards.

As we fought, I made a note of his strengths and weaknesses, a trick that Archie had taught me during our daily lessons in Kildrummy. Everyone had gathered now, gathered to watch Dugald and I battle as if they were at a cock-fight.

Archie and Alex stood side by side, smug grins on their faces, as we circled each other, I waited for the first move.

"First tae draw blood?" I queried nonchalantly.

Dugald looked startled at the forthright question. Sneaking an aiding look at my two guardians, he simply nodded.

I was the first to lunge. Feinting to the right, I swung *Crà* up above my head and around to meet Dugald, who easily parried with his sword. Sweeping to his left, my longsword clashed with vehemence as the tips met and shrugged each other off. Catching me out, he unexpectedly struck low at my feet, cunningly sneaking upwards before completely swerving around and swinging from my defenceless side.

There was no way that I could possibly win against this brute of a man—he seemed too crafty in his manner. But in his latest move towards the middle of my torso, he had left his shield arm vulnerable, giving me the opportunity to strike when all hope had seemed lost.

He lunged forward, heaving his sword arm around to slice my shoulder. I feigned a fall at the last moment, leaving open air to strike and a small body to stumble over. Although his advantage was his wily mind, his physique let him down. Tripping over my body, he moved to steady himself and found nothing but a faceful of dirt. I slid myself out from under his monster of a belly and made a swift incision into his arm, drawing out small globules of burgundy blood.

"Congratulations, my princess," he slurred, exhausted. His relief in not having hurt his princess was written plainly across his face.

"Thank ye for such a pleasurable match," I replied, ecstatic that I'd beaten a fully grown man.

The onlookers gradually dispersed, leaving me in the presence of Archibald, Alexander, and Walter. Dugald had wandered off, making a somewhat pathetic excuse about being needed in the fields.

The sky was coloured a bright blue, hinting at the fact that it looked to be midday already. Soon the men and children would gather in the main street, eagerly listening to the relay of news from Edinburgh while voraciously feasting on their designated rations. News had come in only a week ago of the Tyrant's death, which had taken place over two months ago. This was because nowadays, few messengers journeyed back and forth to the capital, and many of those brave souls had been mercilessly killed on their way back by bandits.

Do not doubt that I was pleased at the arrival of this report, for anyone could tell you that I spent the night celebrating and dancing by firelight while all the men drowned their happiness in freshly brewed ale. No one could have been happier than me. The man whom I had vowed to kill was dead and never coming back, but now we had a bigger problem on our hands: the heir Edward.

Rumours had quickly snaked their way around the country that Edward was planning an alliance with France, a smart move to make if you wished to gain more followers and upturn Scotland. He would no doubt make haste to quicken his French wife with child and put their stupid offspring on the throne. That child would give Scotland decades more harassment from England if he continued his grandfather's ways.

But England had not yet a king. Edward was without a crown and his country without a leader. England would be in turmoil, up in arms and defenceless, so why had my father chosen to rid Scotland of the Comyn clan and not Edward?

"Marjorie," Bishop Lamberton sighed, a faraway look on his face. "Ye know when men go out tae a tavern and have a few pints of ale, they don't really come back the same person? Like something is different, or something is missing?"

I nodded, understanding.

"That is what happened tae yer father one night, the night that he did something really, really bad. A sin that God would nae permit. Now, do ye know the Ten Commandments?"

"Aye, ye taught me all about them a few summers ago," I said, scratching my head as I tried to recall what they were.

"What is the sixth commandment, Marjorie?" he asked, placing an open palm on the top of his desk.

"Thou shalt not kill," I answered confidently, waiting for his nod of approval.

It did not come. "That is correct. This is where yer father comes into the story, so listen carefully, for I shall only repeat this once. When Robert held only the title of earl, he began tae compete for the right tae the throne of Scotland. His competitor—John Comyn, lord of Badenoch and nephew of King John Balliol.

"Comyn had more of a right tae the throne than yer father did, so an agreement was made between the both of them. Yer father's lands were taken by Comyn, but in return, John made sure Robert got the crown. It seemed tae good tae be true—and evidently, it was.

"Comyn told King Edward of England of the agreement between him and yer father. Comyn was rewarded sufficiently for his efforts and sent off for yer father, who once fought under Edward's banner tae avenge the lands taken by Balliol. Robert was taken tae court and ordered tae be executed the next morn. Yer father escaped with the help of a cousin, and he fled, riding for nigh on fifteen days towards the border.

"Now, just a few months before yer father's coronation, a meeting was arranged between him and Comyn, who still believed that Robert didnae know of his treachery. They met inside the Greyfriars church, and from there everything began tae heat up. Comyn was accused of treachery and of betraying the pact they had made, and that was when Robert struck him. Stabbed in the stomach, Comyn fell onto the altar, bleeding. Yer father then left, and two of his closest allies finished Comyn off, also murdering Comyn's uncle.

"News spread quickly, and yer father gained enemies as fast as ye could blink. Not only was King Edward against him, but the whole of the Comyn clan, the Roman church and the pope. He was damned and excommunicated after that incident."

I could not believe what I was hearing. My father, my gentle, loving, tender father had murdered a man out of rage and drunken stupor. Such idiocy! No wonder he left to seek penance; I would have done the same.

Father had never mentioned Comyn, although I had heard reports of his death, for gossip was everything to servants.

"Thank ye, Bishop," I smiled wearily. "I vow to keep this knowledge private."

"Anytime, Marjorie," he replied, turning back to his ink pot and blank canvas pages. Scrawling away on the papers, I stumbled out of the room hurriedly.

"More?" Alexander queried, slanting his half-empty flagon towards me. I shook my head wildly, rolling my tongue around inside my mouth to rid myself of the bittersweet taste.

"Preferably not," I replied half-heartedly. Nodding, he tilted his head back and swigged the rest of his drink.

We were sitting around the glaring fire, gluttonously eating cooked game off of a wooden tray. Walter sat to my right, scraping his sword with a sizzling piece of coal and not once taking his eyes off of it. Sorcha's head rested on the round bulge of Aileen's abdomen; the little girl up above us.

Archibald sat beside Alexander, guzzling his ale in between glancing intently at his wife, his piercing eyes guarding her every move.

"I think it will be a lass," Archibald said suddenly, causing a mob of heads to look up at him.

"Nae, 'tis a lad. I'm sure," Aileen countered, a smug grin on her face.

Archie scowled. "How can ye be so sure?"

Shrugging, Aileen replied. "A mother's instincts."

The silence returned swiftly. It was all too quiet; something had to be amiss. Turning to Walter, I tried to strike up conversation.

"Would ye like me to help ye with that?" I said, eyeing the sword he grasped so tightly in his hands.

He turned to face me, a dark glare shooting out from his flinty eyes. "Nae, my lady. I do nae need yer help or anyone else's for that matter!"

Shocked, I could only watch as he stood up and stormed off into the darkening forest, leaving no trail.

"What was that about?" I asked, knowing that it would be nothing minor. Walter never got angry at minor problems.

"Marjorie," Alexander explained, "a message was sent to yer father from Tormod MacLeod, asking permission for ye tae be married tae Malcolm after this was over. He accepted."

"I beg yer pardon?" I whispered, exasperated and completely confused. There was no way in this life that I was going to marry *that* little bastard. There was no way that my father would make me marry him.

Alexander put his head in his hands, shaking his head slowly. "I'm so sorry, Marjorie."

I sunk down to my knees, my life turning a bleak grey before my eyes. "There is nothing we can do?"

"Nae, nothing," he sulked, his regretful eyes meeting mine.

No one spoke again for the rest of the night, instead letting the cool, swelling air blow the fire out. We shivered in the night, a reminder of the maelstrom that my life was about to become.

Through the night, I swore that I could hear the soft, eerie laughter of Tormod MacLeod echoing through the air, knowing the living Hell that I was striding so easily into. He knew that he had had his wish granted.

Marjorie Bruce

15th of September, 1307

I had not talked to Walter since the message had been received.

After that night in the woodlands, everything had began to turn dull and grey. My senses weren't as sharp, and my heart as numb, aching with every thought that entered my mind. I did not talk to anyone, for the fear of striking out at them was close. I didn't blame them for my father's decisions; how could I?

Training with Archie was the least of my worries. I could not face Malcolm and Tormod MacLeod, let alone Walter; so I did not show. I collected my own water for those five days, cooked my own pottage, washed my own clothes. I did not need ladies-maids doing it all for me, and that is why I would never be able to sit and smile next to Malcolm, knowing that I was imprisoned and only being used to carry his seed. I had to be of use.

For those five days, everyone stayed out of my way. I was not approached by anyone; for they knew that I wanted to be alone. I took Ciaran out for a ride regularly to release my anger.

On the sixth day, I decided to come back to the village. Tying Ciaran up to a tree on the border of the woods, I walked towards the fields lithely. Nothing had changed, and everyone was attending to their usual business as I approached. Archibald was in the fields as usual, the grimace on his face matching the strokes he swiftly made with his sword. Aileen stood happily next to him, one hand resting on her stomach and the other making gestures that seemed to relate to the conversation they were having.

The children did not seem to be in training and were nowhere in sight, so I cautiously walked over to Archibald and Aileen. As they saw me marching through the grain, Archie dropped his sword, and Aileen ran to embrace me. His mouth was tightly closed, but his eyes twinkled—or I seemed to think they did—with relief.

"We thought ye'd never speak tae us again!" Aileen squealed as she held me close to her body.

"I didnae either," I replied, my voice muffled against her shoulder.

When Aileen released me, Archibald dropped to his knees and grabbed my shoulders. "Before anyone else sees ye, we need to speak."

With a glance at Aileen, she too kneeled on the grass below her feet and balanced herself.

"Aye," she agreed. "The prospect of marrying into the slimy family of the MacLeod's is not one I'd wish upon any lady in this kingdom, let alone yerself."

I listened, knowing quite well the lecture I was about to receive.

Archibald continued, "Ye love yer father, no?" I nodded. "Yer father loves ye with all his heart, like no other. No wife, no mistress could ever replace the love a father feels for his child. I may not be a father yet, but I already feel an eternal love for the bairn inside of my darling Aileen. "

Aileen smiled and caressed her stomach. "The argument that Archibald is trying to prove is that yer father loves ye eternally, and he would never put ye in harm's way or do anything he didnae think was right for ye."

She continued softly, aware of passersby, "We do not know what will become of ourselves, Marjorie. Forgive my words, but if the Lord chooses for Malcolm to die in battle before ye wed, so be it. Yer father might one day meet the lad and decide that he is not to be yer husband. There are always chances."

"If I had the choice, I wouldnae marry Malcolm MacLeod," I said to Aileen calmly. "But we all must make sacrifices for the greater good. That is what me father wants, and I must honour his request in the meantime."

"Aye." Aileen nodded, her smile grim. "I was once betrothed, and now my life has completely and utterly changed. For the better, however."

They both stood and placed their arms around each other like hopeless romantics. My thoughts shifted immediately to Walter, whom I decided that I needed to see at once.

"Where can I find Walter?" I asked Archibald.

"I think ye'll find the lad out near the horses," Archibald replied. "He had planned on going hunting with some of the older men later, but I daresay his mind will nae longer linger on that when he has heard that ye have returned."

I grinned and began to walk towards the edge of the forest where the horses were tethered. "Thank ye, and I'll return in time for supper."

I found Walter alone, sitting atop Ciaran, exactly where I had left him minutes earlier. The midday sun had been and gone, and now the sun of the afternoon shone brilliantly through his red hair. The stallion flicked his tail every few moments, amusing Walter.

"Ciaran has been treating ye well, I trust?" I spoke, loud enough for him to hear.

He might have jumped ten feet in the air if Ciaran had not also moved, prompting him to hold tight.

"Marjorie, you're back." He grimaced, sliding feet first off of the horse.

"Aye," I said as I walked over to him, clasping Ciaran's soft mane in one hand and Walter's flimsy shoulder in the other. "I have had a good amount of time tae ponder on some matters."

"And?" Walter pushed, his head angling up for an answer as he was still not yet taller than me.

"I must follow me father's orders. He is the king, Walter," I said slowly, and Walter's head hung like a disgraced man's. "This is not to say that I *want* to wed Malcolm, do trust me in saying that."

Walter nodded, his head still lowered. "He may die in battle, that much I hope for."

"Aye," I said. "I will do whatever I can to put ye in me father's favour. However, in the end, it is his decision."

"Aye," he agreed. "Ye dinnae have tae wed for many years yet, anyway."

"This is true, so shall we forget about the future and live for the moment that is before us right now?" I smiled, my heart pounding with relief and hope.

Jumping back upon Ciaran, he offered me his hand, which I gladly took, and then set off across the fields and into the afternoon sun. The light was almost blinding as Ciaran galloped through the grain and into the open grazing paddocks. The soil was not yet dry from the previous night's rain, and so the splashes of mud made their way onto my garments for good measure.

The feeling of riding takes my breath away. I feel so free that I could almost fly, fly far away from this war-ravaged country and into the arms of my father, whom I have not seen for the past one and a half years. The feeling of riding overpowers the loneliness I feel, hiding just below the surface. I have had no contact with blood relations, and it seems to me that these people I spend my days with have become my kin.

Archie has been with me since the very beginning, a protector who has kept his vow to my father to keep me safe. Sorcha, a sibling that I had longed for since I was a wee bairn, a sibling who had answered all my childhood prayers. Alexander, who has been there for me alongside Archie, and has never failed to amuse me. Aileen, who has become the mother I never had, and Walter, darling Walter, who knows me and my character like the back of his own hand. I am grateful for all of them, and there never seemed to be a dull moment in this makeshift family of mine.

Marjorie Bruce

THE END

About the Author

Emmerson Brand is a high school student living in Perth, Western Australia with her family. Her love of writing from an early age combined with an interest in her own family genealogy and history inspired her to create *Spirit of Fire* - a first person historical account of the Scottish Wars of Independence. She hopes to continue a career in writing and one day explore her ancestral home ground for herself.

Lightning Source UK Ltd.
Milton Keynes UK
UKHW011945080321
380016UK00012B/1610/J